Coven 82

Skull County Series

BOOK ONE OF THREE

A Tale By Lacie Barg'e

The story which you are about to read contains some fact.

Names and places have been changed for their protection.

Due to the high amounts of witchcraft in the United States and other countries, most things such as spells, castings, and divinations have been protected in this story.

If you desire to learn more of the dark arts of the craft, beware, you might not ever come back normal (and that is not a joke).

Remember where your heart is and always use your head.

Happy Reading....

This book is dedicated to **<u>God</u>**

and to those who prayed for me through wicked times

Thank you for your compassion to save me

and bring me back to the "light"

May God Bless you and keep you safe

XOXOX

Chapter One

CLOSE TO THE END

Ava and her husband were sitting by Betty's bedside as she was dying. Ava was Betty's childhood best friend even though Betty fell into a dark and horrible lifestyle. Betty was pale and her face was bruised and burnt from a suicide attempt. Her neck was severely rope burned and weeping yellowish red discharge from where gauze had covered up the nasty wound.

Ava's husband read from his bible some passages about walking through the valley of death. Ava held her friends hand with tears swelling in her eyes. Betty was holding on to every breath she took. A nurse walked in casually to check the stats on Betty's condition.

"How bad is it? Did the blood work show any signs of drug usage?" Ava asked.

"Well, she does have some internal bleeding from the fall. Her blood test results show signs of methamphetamine and some drinking. We are doing the best we can." The nurse said with some panic in her voice.

"Our medical insurance will cover this right?" Ava asked the nurse.

"Not to worry. Treatment will be covered." The nurse gave a strained smile.

"Ava..." Betty came out of her haziness. "Ava, I need to tell you."

"Betty." Ava rushed to her friend's bedside. "You shouldn't try to talk okay. Trent is here. We are here for you sweetie." Ava held Betty's hand again; caressing it with tender thoughts like a mother would do for a child.

"Pastor Trent." Betty said with a smile. "That is funny. Never thought it would end like this. You went to elementary school with me. I still see you as a child you know." Betty tried to laugh but ended up coughing with pain. She squeezed Ava's hand.

"Betty." Is all Ava could say to her.

"Look." Betty said with wheezing, "I really need to tell you what I have done. I don't want to die without telling you." Her eyes rolled back and she started coughing again. The next words were a struggle to say but she managed to speak them. "I want to have my conscience cleared of my sins before I go. Please listen to me, I beg you, please." It was as though God had his hand on Betty at this moment and she was clear of most of her pain so that she could tell her sins to Trent and Ava.

Trent put his bible down and softly told Betty, "We are here to listen to Betty."

Betty then released the tension grip from Ava's hand. "Remember our high school days at Skull High? It was during the last two weeks before school was over. I was expelled along with a few others in the group I hung out with that year. Remember?"

1993, May 20th, Skull High School. The year of grunge music, parties, and knowing where a teenager stood in adulthood. Or so we all thought. Ava was President of The Homemakers of America and Trent was the secretary for that club. Betty was just friends with everyone and wild as a March hare with her wild sporadic outfits and attitude. Even though she was friends with everyone, she mainly hung out with the misfits who would meet in the library at lunch time or ditch during the first couple of classes. They dressed in flannel shirts, ripped up jeans, combat boots, and black shirts. They were also known as stoners.

Betty came to school late as usual with her close friend Layla. Betty always showed up late with bruises or red marks on her face or arms. It was nothing unusual. Her father always beat her and everyone knew it. Nothing could be done about the abuse in Betty's home because her father was so well known in the community and people covered it up like nothing was going on. Betty and Layla were in the lower restroom putting on makeup and preparing to enter their classes late. Ava came from French class to use the restroom and found the two girls giggling as they shared a cigarette. They were putting on makeup as they handed the cigarette back and forth to one another. Both of them were dressed in black tight jeans, black V cut neck short sleeved shirts and an old flannel around their waists. Layla spilled some facial powder on her left combat boot and bent over to wipe the pale powder off.

"Hello Ava." Layla said with a wicked grin, she didn't even look up from what she was doing. It gave Ava the creeps.

"Layla." Ava smiled back. She approached them with concern for they were smoking. "Oh Betty he hit you again didn't he?" Ava put her hand on her friends shoulder. Betty and Ava used to live next door to each other when they were in elementary school. They hung out until now when Betty started hanging out with misfits, the stoners.

"I'll be fine Ava." Betty said coldly as she shrugged her friends hand from off her shoulder. "Like it's never happened before, shit. You take things so dramatically." Betty giggled trying to cover up how she truly felt. "A little makeup and it's gone. See?" Betty stared into the mirror at Ava's reflection.

"The jerk should be beat up himself by a big giant penis." Layla laughed out loud and Betty laughed at the joke with her. Layla was rummaging around in her big over sized book bag and stood up with a can of hair spray. The cigarette was hanging from her painted red lips.

"Well," Ava said in a more businesslike manner. "If you think so." Ava thought it was childish behavior anyway and she came to the restroom for more important matters. She headed off into a dull green stall and did her business of taking a tinkle.

"Miss Preppy anyway. She has not a clue what you go through at home." Layla whispered to Betty. "The only thing she knows about is her pom poms and jock boyfriends." Layla smiled at Betty and rolled her eyes. The two girls giggled at that. Although deep down Betty didn't tell Layla that Ava knew about her life at home. She didn't want to tell Layla that because reputations were on the line. Or so she thought.

The two girls headed off in separate directions, Ava close behind Betty who was dragging her feet in dread to enter a classroom late. "Betty wait up!" Ava called.

"Ava you really need to keep your mouth shut about us." Betty wasn't really mad at her friend but mad at herself.

"You shouldn't care what others think." Ava said back. "But if you really feel that way. Geez he really hit you hard today didn't he?" She stopped Betty to look at the somewhat covered red spot on her face. It was turning purple through the thick make up.

"Well, I am concerned." Ava then started up towards French class. "If you ever need a true friend let me know. I'll always be there for you."

Betty lagging behind to get to French class as well yelled back to Ava, "Sure I'll remember that on my death bed okay!"

Betty entered the class with a silence. She was fifteen minutes late. The teacher was used to her tardiness and therefore gave her a slip to go down to the office. Ava smiled and winked with a giggle. Betty rolled her eyes and left the classroom in fashionable routine. She went back outside and crumpled up the tardy slip. Threw it in her bag and slowly headed down towards her locker. Layla would be down soon as well with her tardy slip. It was never ending.

"Betty." Trent said. "What does this mean? What does this situation have in tie with sinning?" He looked at Betty's repulsive mutilated face with concern trying to search for some hidden clue in her puffy blood shot eyes.

"It has everything to do with why I am here." Betty stared into his eyes, penetrating his very soul with an evil chill. "That is the day I met him. The one, Menod Natsatis."

Ava stared at her now husband with confusion. Trent looked at Ava thinking in his mind that may be Betty was losing it completely before she died. His eye contact went from Ava back to Betty. Betty was staring hard at Ava, and then rolled her eyes in a creepy way back to Trent.

"Listen to me, they are out there waiting. I know it, I can feel them." Betty said gasping. "You have to help me Trent. You are of God. You can help drive it out of me. Please just listen." she closed her eyes and remembered the rest of that day.

Layla. Light brown curly hair. Long and pinned up in a loose bun. Loose trendils of hair cascading around her face and neck. Green eyes, like a cat. Surrounded with thick black eye liner and trimmed with long lashes with heavy mascara. Skin was pale, slightly freckled. Flawless. Legs like those of a model, hips shapely under tight black fashionable jeans. Breasts; perky and full under a black tee shirt. Cleavage perfect from where the V line on the shirt started, black laced bra slightly showing by the shoulder. She smelled like vanilla and roses. A crescent moon in abalone shell hung from a silver chain around her neck and it dangled in the hollow where the collar bone meets in the middle of her chest. She was ravishing in beauty.

"So, what are we to do today?" Layla said to the small group of misfit friends as they sat in the local mini mart waiting to go back to the school. "Hello? Betty? Earth to Betty!" She laughed.

"Sorry. Just a bit stoned. Hah." Betty tried to laugh. Her stare went from Layla to the traffic outside the window. "We could go to my place."

"And wait for your dad to come home? I think not." Layla said in a snotty tone. "Hey Allen, what do you think? What should we do today?"

Allen was your class act nerd. Tow head blond

typical large nosed geek with nothing better to do but drive his rich parents into debt. "We could steal Dawson's car again and go joy riding. That was fun." He had this Beavis and Butthead attitude about him. He even laughed like Beavis and Butthead.

"Absolutely not." This was Gerald. For short we called him Grunt. Not sure why but we did. "I really don't want my parents to bale me out of trouble. Shit." He was sitting on one side of Layla and Allen sat on the other. Betty was across the three.

"Good thing your family is part of the court system," Allen went on, "or the four of us would be in jail right now and not ditching classes." He laughed that annoying laugh again. Grunt reached over Layla and hit Allen over the head then proclaimed, "Let's go swimming in that old guy's pool!"

"Icky and be stared at by him and his freak lover?" Layla grossed out. "I say we get J Dog and go out to those cliffs we'd been meaning to hike up to." She looked at Allen as Allen had his hand on her thigh. "You are so brave little boy." Her smile was smoldering but had a hint of warning to it.

"Sorry." Allen quickly removed his hand, placed it in his lap with the other hand and stared directly down at the table.

"J Dog? Why him? We'd have to go back to campus and drag his big ass out of class. No. I say we go ourselves. He'll just slow us down." Grunt said with anger.

"J Dog has the map numb nut. We can't go without a map." Layla said in an angry tone back. She was messing around with her bracelets that covered up some cuts on her left wrist.

"What are you guys talking about?" Betty said. "Map? I hate J Dog. Cliffs? Hiking? Dagga I'm thirsty." Betty felt more stoned than usual. Strange, heavy and very dry. She stumbled out from the booth they sat in and went to the soda fountain to get a drink but the tunnel vision made it harder than usual. Layla, Grunt, and Allen looked at each other and laughed out loud. "Yeah, laugh you freaks." Betty said loudly. "You laced the weed I know it."

"We didn't lace cranky spanks Betty." Allen said. "You are just under a little spell." He laughed annoyingly.

"Blow it Allen." Layla groaned. "Really want her to know don't you?" She reached up and twisted his ear lope.

"No. I thought you already told her?" Allen sneered.

"No." Layla growled. She released his ear and pushed his head. His long surfer cut style stick straight hair flew about his vision like waves of soft straw. He brushed it out of his face.

Betty went to the counter and gave the cashier some money. Somehow every word her friends were saying echoed like an empty steel room in her head. "Shit you guys need to shut up. That or talk softer." Betty smiled at the clerk who glared at her for the foul language. Betty, slowly and carefully as not to trip on her own two feet, walked back to the booth and sat down with a clumsy thud spilling some soda on the table. "Spell? Okay. As God as my witness." She laughed hard putting her hand over her face and looking at her friends. "I have no God. What the hell are you three do'n? We smoked some bad weed. Picked it fresh from the skanky orchard." Betty was laughing so hard she felt insane.

"Undo it Allen!" Layla gritted her teeth. "We are all going to get into trouble if you don't undo it."

Allen was laughing at Layla's anger. "No you skank," Allen laughed, "you undo it."

"Undo it or I'll come up with something so darn horrible your mother will die." Layla warned. Her eyes were turning a lime green. Betty watched Layla's eyes and out of fear she laughed even harder. She couldn't stop and it hurt.

"Give me what I want Layla and I'll do it." Allen gave an evil wicked grin. He licked his lips.

"Fine." Layla was fierce but surrendered. "Well, we are waiting?" Layla was frustrated.

Allen grabbed Betty's head. She was still laughing uncontrollably. He got so close to her face with his and whispered "Tes, doma, kelato."

Betty stopped abruptly. She went from cracking up and feeling super stoned to straight faced. Her eyes jetted around in fear. "What the hell was that about?" Betty was completely sober and clear in the head despite the fact she had smoked two eights of green bud about an hour ago.

She smiled in some sort of realization. "That was damn awesome. I want to know more." Betty was eager with anticipation.

"Great Allen. You are so dumb." Layla crossed her arms and rolled her eyes.

"What is it you want to know Betty?" Grunt asked her.

"What the hell kind of illusion you had me in?" Betty said.

"Look." Grunt said looking around like there might

be spies. "It isn't an illusion." He cleared his throat. "It is just a state of mind. You were subjected to laugh like a crazy woman. You were deluded with Allen's pranks." Grunt shot a cold stare at Allen. "He likes you."

Allen reached over Layla to hit Grunt but Layla grabbed his wrist and twisted it before he got a hit in.

"Then why am I sober after smoking all that green leafy?" Betty snarled. "I'm going back to class, I shouldn't even be here. You guys are weird sometimes you know? One minute we are all pretty cool friends and then just like this, I am in the dark about things." Betty got up, picked up her back pack and started to leave.

Layla shouted at Betty as Betty was leaving the mini mart. "Get J Dog for us. Please Betty Cat?"

"Sure." and Betty was off into the blackberry bush trail and over a fence back to school. She was clouded by the mystery of almost dying of laughter. They had to have laced the pot with something. May be the pot they smoked was just placebo. Her mind was racing. Then she heard movement behind her. In fear of getting caught before third period class was over, she quickly scurried towards some scrub oak by the gym. She hunkered down and waited. Her heart pumped fast. Sweat rolled off her forehead. It could be the Vice

Principle on his quest to suspend and expel those who were outcasts of the popular group of kids.

The shadow came near. Too tall to be the Vice. Too skinny for that matter. Betty's anxiety attack came to a halt. The Vice was short and stout. It was Allen who followed her back. "Allen." Betty called to him as he came into vision. "You are an ass."

Allen had seen Betty sitting under the bush. "And you are in a sticker bush. Who is the bigger ass?" He joined her. Sat on the dirt ground and lit up a cigarette. "So, are we waiting for break?"

"I guess." Betty said disappointed. "Wish I was stoned." She lit up a cigarette as well.

"Careful what you wish for." Allen's eyes were clever. "Here take this." He fished out of his back pack a sleek black book. "Read it tonight and join me there."

"Um," Betty was confused. "Join you where?" She asked.

"You'll see." Allen said with a sweet smile.

Betty took the book with her free hand. She opened it up and started to look over its contents. "Allen. What is this?" She asked.

"What does it say?" He asked back.

"In the beginning the Goddess Hasbrath created darkness. In the darkness she pricked her finger to draw about the blood within and she threw out into the universe a dazzle of stars. Hasbrath created all life and life created an equal of the opposite named Menod Natsatis. He created light by impregnating Hasbrath with the Son. Menod Natsatis then began to take over as King of the universe and Hasbrath was at his side as Queen." Betty kept reading this black book of what seemed like fairytales. When she came to the end she read out loud, "Hasbrath's betrayal to her King, the one she birthed from all of nature was forgiven after her cruel death by their children guardians. Menod Natsatis is now looking for Hasbrath in those that we call the femme." She closed the book. "And this is what? You get the weirdest literature." She took a drag of her cigarette and put it out.

"You can see it?" Allen was quite amazed.

"I could see that this is strange. I'll join you. But where?" Betty agreed but asked again.

"Just read this book tonight and follow its directions okay. I'll call you." He said putting out his cigarette and cranked his head towards hers. Betty gazed into his soft blue eyes and then shut them and entered the moment of a kiss. Lips touched gently. Tongues glided into each other, taunting, pleasing, and her fingers traced his jawbone. The kiss got more intense with her touch. He slipped his hands over her hips to move her closer to him. Inside Betty's head became fuzzy and light. His mouth tasted like sickly sweet candy. Jolly Ranchers. Hhhmm. What flavor? Watermelon, no. Cherry? Apple, yes. So sweet.

She felt her shirt go up and his hand slid under it. He fingered the edge of her padded bra right under her right breast. His other hand lightly raked the small of her bare back. They were starting to make out under the scrub oak next to the gym. Then the darn bell rang for break. He broke away from the kiss. "I have to find J Dog. Later Betty." His eyes twinkled in delight. Betty was left in a daze of sexual arousal.

She just sat there, looking at the sleek black book. She rubbed the hard leather cover with her thumb. Then she stuck it in her bag. It must have been twenty minutes before she started to get up and WHAM that greedy Vice Principle was right around that corner.

"Miss Ditching Betty." The Vice smirked.

"Ditching? The bell is gonna ring for class in like five minutes." She said in a hot tone.

"Not for you. You are going with me and you are telling me where your friends are." He said with a terrible shit eating grin.

"Whatever. I'm going to class." She said ignoring

his stance.

"Then you are expelled from this school." He said threatening.

"You can't do that! I don't even know where they are!" Betty said as she quickly walked towards her fourth period class.

"You've been with them all day today so don't lie to me missy." He grabbed her arm.

"Look, I don't need your shit or any other guys okay Mr. Egghead so take your paws off me!" She yelled.

Chapter 2

Some on lookers hurrying to class were watching as they ran by. Betty glared at him with hot pokers shooting out her brown eyes. "Expel me, I dare you." and she trotted off to class. When she entered class, not five minutes went by and the Vice Principle was taking her down to the office to expel her. She was sent home.

THE FOREST

"So," Betty said to her father, "You have nothing to say about this? You are going to let them expel me from school?"

"Yep. You are a no good rotten teenager." He said in a drunken mad tone. "You have no real interest in educating yourself. Why waste my time and effort on a loser like you?" He sat down on the filthy couch. He put his drink in front of him on the coffee table and turned on the large screened television. He ignored her.

"In two more weeks school will be over. I won't finish my junior year of high school dad!" Betty yelled.

"You can't just let them do this! I wasn't ditching damn you! Are you listening to me?" She got right in front of the television. "Do something!" she screamed in his face.

Her dad stared right through her as if she was transparent. Then out of nowhere, as if she was a fly, his fist went flying out from his lap and Betty went down onto the floor. Now the other side of her face started to swell up like a balloon. His attention was still on the television.

"You messed up drunken stubborn fat ass slob piece of shit!" Betty yelled. "You will regret this night." and she went up stairs and slammed her door. Her father turned up the volume of the television drowning out any noise that may or may not come from her room upstairs.

Usually Betty would turn on her stereo, blasting out his precious television. This time was different. Instead, she took out the black book that Allen gave her. She started to read it. These writings and tales were older than the druids. They were of magic, but not just any form of magic. Something was amiss with this. The book itself seem to be alive and she felt as though the book was absorbing her every thought and emotion. She set up her room like the directions said. A single black candle on a pedestal. A comfortable blanket to kneel on. An offering cup made of silver. She waited for Allen's phone call.   Allen never called. Betty fell asleep until her alarm clock chimed off ten minutes until midnight. She got up from out of her bed covers. She kneeled in front of the candle. Opened the book, lit the candle and rehearsed the prayer with not a doubt in her heart. As soon as midnight hit, the prayer chant was over and she felt her body transgress into a place that wasn't her bedroom. The feeling was like being sucked into a fleshy opening and she entered into a passage way without moving. The passage way came to her through that strangely written prayer. She opened her eyes and blew out the candle like the instructions had said. She was in a forest meadow. Trees, tall and strange surrounded her. The sky was like dark thick fog and the sunlight tried to burn its way through. The meadow grass was thick and tall, abnormally thick like fleshy fingers, soft, green, and warm touching her bare legs. The rumbling earthquake came from behind like the book had mentioned it would. She dared not to turn and face it, like the instructions said.

Her heart raced, her body trembled with fear. The sound came fast and suddenly stopped right behind her. So close, she could feel heat. "Do you fear me Betty?" A wicked deep voice asked.

"I fear you my Lord." Betty said. She was bowing her body as in an offering. Still, she didn't turn around. The book stated not to look at him unless he offers. He poured some sort of wine into the silver cup. It was crimson in color. It looked almost jewel like, sparkling in the dim light.

"You offer yourself to me. Drink Betty." He said to her. She drank the strange wine but kept her head down and forward facing the empty meadow. The wine tasted sweet like exotic fruit and yet acidic like blood "Your friends are all here." He said to her. "They have been waiting. Rise Betty and join them."

"Yes my Lord." As Betty stood up she noticed that she was naked. A bit ashamed, she covered up her middle with her arms.

"No need to feel shame. In the beginning there was no shame with Hasbrath. This is your rebirth Betty. You'll need a new name. You are now a creature unto my world and Betty there stays there. The Betty here will become evolved. Kneel my servant before me."

"Yes my Lord." Betty said. She turned around without looking directly at him. She kneeled at his feet. His feet were normal, like a man. Her every thought was being read and she felt it.

"I'm quite the same as a human." He reassured her. "You are now proclaimed as Reziah. Rise Reziah and join your friends."

Betty; the now Reziah, came up from kneeling position and seen Allen, Layla, Grunt and others that hung out at school with her. Allen slipped a black robe around her naked body and welcomed her with her new name. The dark and wicked voice of what seem to be man walked away into the rising mist, naked.

"Is this a good time to call?" Allen smiled.

"What is this? Is this a dream?" Betty was full of questions.

"No." Grunt said. "Do not question anything Reziah. Accept it like you would a gift."

"Do the others know who I am here?" She asked again, ignoring Grunts request to accept this gift.

"Not really." He said. "They are just followers. You might not remember. You cannot go around knowing you know when you go back. There is much work to be done for you. Come and join the rest of the others."

"There are others?" Betty said in astonishment.

"Eighty five covens and we all meet here every night." Layla said taking Betty by the arm and leading her into the forest mist, out of the meadow. They came to a soft padded dirt path. Her senses were very acute to the surroundings. Many voices came from the edges of the mist. Whispering voices, soft and feathery entered her hearing.

"They are here to welcome you as a new comer of our coven." Layla said.

"Where are they?" Betty asked as they walked upon the dirt path.

"Look around you and you will see them." Layla said with a hand jester reaching out in front of them. There in the dim light were people standing in the shadows of the trees, bowing to Betty like a queen. Many young and many old. The two girls were approaching a stone platform where the sky opened up through the cathedral of trees. "Go up and say your new name so that all can hear." Layla said releasing Betty's arm.

Betty got up onto the platform. She peered around her and the people in the shadows gathered around to hear her. "Reziah". She said it loudly and with a form of pride. The people around her repeated it back to her. She watched the people bow at her. They chanted to her in a welcome like fashion. Then Layla helped her down from the stone platform which had odd carvings of symbols around the edges. Allen and Grunt spent a great deal of time talking and instructing Betty about where she was, the book, and the new found religion.

Allen handed Betty a beautiful stone, the shade of blue like his eyes. It was clear like glass and felt like liquid on her fingertips. Smooth and cool. In it she seen images dancing and the dim light made the small stone glitter and twinkle. "This will help you when you need it. No harm will touch you again." He kissed her forehead as if she was a child. Betty was beginning to have a fondness of Allen.

Betty must have been in that forest all night with her friends and new found friends of foreign regions. Then the doorway shut like a time warp going backward. She awoke on her bed like it was just all a dream. A single stone, which was given to her by Allen, lay in the palm of her hand like a key to go back each night. Even though it was like a dream. It was very real like the stone in her hand. She fondled the stone and peered into it. The dancing images were not there but it caught the dawn light and glittered and twinkled with a form of curiosity. She sat up from her bed and stared out the window. Today felt much different than all the other days in her life. Looking about her room, everything felt like this reality was a dream and that her dream was reality. In realization, this world was artificial.

The candle and pedestal with the blanket still lay out on her floor. The candle was unburned, as if she never did it. But with the stone in her hand, she knew she did. She came back with something. She picked up the make shift alter and fumbled through the black book for more instructions. Today, since there was no school anymore, she was going out on a hike. A hike that would bring about a new alter like the book instructed her to make. She read about the man figure that she feared, Menod Natsatis. The one who sounded like an earthquake behind her but was quite human in form.

As she went downstairs, her dad was passed out, television still blasting out nonsense sound. He was snoring. Drool dripped from the corner of his mouth. Gross. Betty went into the kitchen, fixed herself a pop tart. Ate it with a glass of milk. With book at hand and stone in pocket, she left outdoors to the neighboring field. She was in search of a grove of trees that would hide her from the nights ahead. Places to set up a stone alter. She hiked for hours until she found the perfect spot. A patch of wide branching oak trees. Six of them. A few protruding rocks in the center. She put a few flat rocks down over a natural made hole. She stuck the book in the hole along with the silver cup. She chanted one of the memorized chants from the book to purify the area. Then she sat there for a moment. She placed the stone on her new alter and fell asleep.

A few days had passed. A school dance was coming up. Allen and she met a lot in that dream forest but this time, she had to meet him at the dance and go to his place for their coven was holding some sort of meeting that night. The whole group of misfits, stoners, would be at the school dance. Now which ones were in the coven was unknown to each other. They would see each other in that forest but forget. Betty knew not to mention it to anyone, not even discuss it with Layla, Grunt or Allen. Menod Natsatis knows and hears all. How she was getting into the dance was beyond her, but somehow she would manage.

Thinking about sneaking in. Heck, she had a book of crafty ideas. She went to her stone alter out in the hills. The perfect spell opened up right out of the book. Betty went gathering certain things the spell asked for. She prepared them, chanted the ritual and went back to wait it out. Her and her dad stopped talking. The television somehow mysteriously blew a tube. He didn't come home from work now until real late from the bar down town. Things seem to be going smoothly in her life. But, in all reality, it was just starting to crumble all around her. As she waited for the evening to begin, she made a pendant necklace for the stone that Allen gave her. Day by day those dancing images became clearer in waking hours as in the dream realm.

Things in the dream realm were amazing to Betty. It was like a miniature familiar place now. A fountain that was dried up but she had felt water in it when it was empty. A brook with the babbling sounds of frightened voices telling her to go back. Faces in the brook appeared and they were screaming silently. A fawn with a human likeness that followed her around when she was in the dream realm. A castle tower with no door or windows but she heard voices inside. A wall that barred the forest. The wall was massively large and could not be jumped, climbed, nor scaled by any human. A giant gate made of rot iron and locked forever. Sometimes when Betty approached this in the dream realm she could see Ava on the other side. The other side was a park with children playing and other familiar people that would get spooked just walking up to the gate.

Ava. Tall. Thin. Blond shoulder length hair. Always wearing a pastel color of pink or purple. Big soft blue eyes. A cross hanging at her neck. It was something her grandmother had given her when she was very young. Her shape was cute but not at all seductive. She was average looking. Ordinary. But, her faith was enticing and rich with God. It used to make Betty envy her, but now it just churned her stomach into a sick feeling. Ava the Christian. Why she would try to talk to Betty? In the dream realm, Betty would approach the gate and Ava stood there trying to help saying things like "Betty, you are stuck. Please find a way out." or "Aren't you afraid of demons? Get out, save your soul Betty." It was nonsense. Betty didn't feel the forest as evil. It was comforting.

Although strange things happened there in that forest. Betty wasn't alarmed by them anymore. Her senses became stronger in the realm of dream and now here in this world. Her powers to make things happen were growing. Allen and she were personally close now in the dream realm. She had amazing unbelievable sexual encounters with Allen. Layla now and again would join them in a lust fest. They had become family in a dark world of their own. Although it had been a week since she last personally seen her friends, things were happening in Betty's life. Things never thought of. The impossible was now obtainable.

She finished making a pendant out of the blue

stone. Silver wire wrapped the stone securely in a decorative manner and hung on a black silk cord. Betty, not of the craft making type, was beginning to become very artistic. Her once stick drawings of people were now life like on paper. She could cook now when before she could only burn bacon and toast. She was quick, like a stealthy cat. Quiet like a mouse. When her dad opened his mouth to slam her down with fowl words, her gaze would cut into him leaving her dad without anything to say. She was able to stay up all night without troubles or drugs and she could sleep peacefully now without tossing and turning. She put the necklace around her neck and tucked it into her shirt. It was time to go to the school dance.

The Vice Principle and some other teachers stood at the glass entryway of the gym. Kids were gathering to enter. Money was being passed about for those who didn't have enough. Chattering and gossip was amongst the crowd. Betty stood tall awaiting her approval to get in. No one noticed her as they took her money and let her enter. The craft of magic worked wonderfully. They actually thought of her as an out of town student. So much for recognition on their part! She went into the dark gym and stood next to the padded wall. She didn't have to squint her eyes to see anything; they adjusted to the darkness and flashing disco lights. She could hear Allen laughing. Layla making fun of some jocks dancing techniques. There, on top of the folded bleachers. They were sitting down smoking cigarettes, as usual.

Betty walked up towards them. They didn't even look at her. She hopped up and sat next to Grunt. "Hey Grunt." She smiled.

"Betty precious. Haven't seen you around for a while. Rumor has it you got expelled?" He said passing his lit cigarette to her.

Betty took a drag and handed it back. "Yes and the idiots let me in tonight." She said over the loud music.

"They are blind freaks and just want your money." Layla said laughing. Allen was laying on Layla's lap looking up at her.

"So," Betty said. "Where is the rest of the crew?" She was looking around for the rest of their friends.

"Over there being stupid retards. Are they requesting disco music again? Someone needs to be spanked." Allen said as he flirted with Layla.

"Come on Grunt," Betty took Grunts arm, "lets request a song and dance a bit. It looks like Layla and Allen have something else planned."

"Yeah and it doesn't include us." Grunt said accepting Betty's offer. The two of them joined their usual crew of misfit stoner friends and danced to The Clash. The night was energetic than usual. More flowing than it was boredom. Allen offered Betty a place to stay and she accepted that. She really didn't want to go home and the fact that there was a coven meeting at 1 am to attend. Their only friend with a car, Dawson, drove everyone home. When he dropped off Allen and Betty he was silent. It gave Betty the creeps.

"What was that about?" Betty asked Allen as they got out of the Jeep. "What is wrong with Dawson?"

"He is in love with Layla and Layla was flirting with me." Allen said. "Everyone is in love with Layla. She can't stop putting beauty spells on herself." He smiled at Betty.

"I thought we aren't supposed to talk about that." Betty said.

"I gave you the book," he said, "so therefore you and I could talk endlessly about it."

"Who else has a book?" Betty said curiously. "I mean, could you tell me?"

"No." Allen said bluntly. "But," he added, "I could tell you who *may* have a book. Not sure if they followed through though." They were walking up to his front porch, which was rickety and old. The door was red; the house was white trimmed in red. The porch light flickered above them. It was ten thirty at night. When they entered the house, his parents were already in bed. His sister and brother were sitting up watching cartoons from the VCR. "Hey you two need to go to bed now." He said to his siblings in a loving tone.

"How was the dance Allen?" His sister asked.

"I'll let you know in the morning okay. Now get to bed and say your prayers." He said to them. Prayers? Allen? Strange, but Betty waved it off like it might have been protocol of some sort.

"Betty," Allen said, "come on, I'll tell you." and he gestured a motion to leave the living room for his room down the hallway. When the bedroom door shut behind them, Allen lit a few candles and sat down on a couch. Betty sat on his bed. "No need to be shy. You can sit with me. I don't bite too hard." He smiled to her.

Betty got up and curled up like a cat on the other end of the couch. "So," She said, "who else has a book?"

"Well," he started, "as you know my dad runs a book making business for covens and witches all around the world. All sorts of spell and magic books. I wasn't interested until this big guy from St. Andrew bought this one type of witch book. He wanted me to recruit people. As you know Layla and Grunt were my first to bring into the coven. The three of us are the Highest Reign, or what you'd call Priests and Priestess."

Betty cut in. "Why you three? Why not three others?"

"It is our birth right. The order of our birth dates align with the universe in a perfect order. There are three others which I know but cannot name. They are higher than us three. They are the Elders. They also have the same alignment as us three. So I have just told you about six members. There *may or may not* be these seven; Jakey Snake, Dinky, Zen, Seth, Corey, Carl, Hattie, Tina, and Stephanie."

"You didn't mention my name?" Betty smiled. "So if I go to that place in my dreams and see these people...."

"You remember the dream?" Allen asked in astonishment.

"You mean dreams as in plural." She stated.

"No, it is just one dream, trust me. Not too many I've talked to remember the dream." He said as he kicked off his black canvas shoes.

"One dream? Like the same dream but continuing?" She asked.

"No, like one dream connected to those in all the covens. In fact the place is quite real. You can actually bring back objects." He said while taking off his black button up shirt and putting on a clean T-shirt.

"Like this stone you gave me." Betty pulled out the stone from under the neckline of her shirt. "What kind of stone is this Allen?"

"Not from this world," he giggled normally and not like beavis. "I found it the first time I went adventuring on my own in that place."

"What are we doing tonight at the coven? If we could meet in a dream, why do we have to meet personally? Also why are there 85 covens?" Betty asked as she got closer to Allen to fix his hair for him. She ran her fingers through his soft straight blond hair.

"Well," He said as he moved from her flirting and handed her the shirt he just took off for her to sleep in, "there are things in this world that don't exist in that one. Have you seen animals there? Or children? So, we meet up about three or four times a month to do things that can't be done there. Tonight there is a sacrifice we must perform. I have to give you a few things and tell you a few rules." He got up from the couch and Betty started to switch shirts. "85 covens are because of the star alignment. We are number 82 in the region." He went to his closet. Grabbed a big black box. Took out a few items and returned. "First of all when the Mister picks you up, you will have to put this on in the car. No clothing or jewelry allowed, just this okay. Wear these shoes; they are more like slippers with tread. Secondly, when you follow the others dressed like you, do not try to look under their hoods of the cloak. That is very important. No one knows who is who and this whole ordeal is of secrecy and loyalty to Menod Natsatis."

Allen handed Betty a black velvet cloak with a large hood. "Naked aye?" She giggled. "I have problems with showing off my body."

Chapter 3

"It won't be a problem after a few rituals like tonight, trust me." He smiled at her in the dim of his candlelit room.

"Do you have a pair of sweat pants?" She asked him.

"Yeah sure." He went to his dresser and pulled out a pair of gray sweat pants and gave them to her to sleep in. "Just to let you know we sacrifice big things and there will be times you will end up messy with blood." He turned around so that she could dress.

"It won't bother me. I'll just imagine it is my dad." She slipped out of her tight black jeans and put on the sweat pants.

He turned around to sit back down on the couch. "What if it is your dad?" Allen looked serious.

"All the merrier." Betty laughed as she snuggled back up into her corner of the couch.

"Get some Z's before we go." Allen said as he put a blanket over her that was on the back of the couch. He set an alarm clock by the side of the couch.

"Thanks Allen." She said. She closed her eyes and fell fast asleep.

Betty awoke to a chiming alarm clock. One of those wind up ones with the big silver bells on either side. The numbers on the alarm clock glowed funky neon green with two arms, one short showing the minutes and the other long showing the hour. She was wide awake. Alive. She grabbed the cloak and shoes that Allen gave her and silently, like a mouse, went out the front door. Grunt, Layla, and Allen prepared her in the dream realm, and she wasn't a bit nervous. She stood outside the gate of Allen's front yard. Waiting for the unknown.

A black car drove slowly by, stopping where she stood. It was a four door Cadillac. Tinted windows except for the front. As if she knew what to do, she got into the back of the car. A man was driving. He had light brown hair, fair skin, and clean shaved. He wore a classic business button up white shirt, black slacks, and shiny black shoes. An everyday ordinary average guy. He didn't look at her in the rear view mirror nor did he talk to her. As soon as she shut the door, he drove onward to their destination.

Betty quickly got undressed in the back seat and put on the cloak. There was a box for her stuff to be put into. She took off her jewelry; a few bracelets, a ring, and she kept the necklace on. She tucked that into the neck folds of the cloak. She was completely naked except for the thick velvet black cloak and funky slipper shoes. She sat there waiting in the silence wondering where the hell they were driving off to. The Mister didn't say a word when Betty lit up a cigarette. There was an open pack laying on the seat. From someone else? Who cared, it was convenient. She watched the smoke being sucked out the cracked window. The night breeze felt soft on her skin.

It must have been about an hour drive of windy road through Skull County. No signs except that of Jesus Maria Road. Funny. The first part of the road sign was Jesus. Betty giggled in amusement. The driver stopped in the middle of nowhere. He finally looked at her almost like a robot. She got the just; she put her hood up, opened the door, and got out of the car. At first she thought she was alone. The Mister drove off into the darkness. She peered around and seen movement. Animal? Cow? No, it was others dressed just like her going through a gate. She followed. The gate was connected to a barbed wire fence. It was for horses and their riders to go in and out of the property that they were entering.

The moon light was shining brightly on them. They looked like shadows moving through a cattle field.

No cows though. Not one in sight anywhere. A few small oak trees, a hill, then over the hill were a creek in a ravine. A bridge. A bit rustic to be crossing but they all managed. Where was Allen? May be that was his pack of cigarettes Betty took a smoke from? She followed the small crowd through a thicket of bush and large rocks after crossing the bridge. A cave. In the pale moon light, there was a reddish yellow glow from a cave entrance. The heat was hitting her like a sauna. Thank the stars she was naked or she would die of heat stroke.

Chanting was mellow but thick coming out of the cave. One by one they entered. She was the third to enter the cave. Instantly, as if she had done all this before, chanting came out of her and the others. Some language that only the thirteen knew of. It was moving, rhythmic, and arousing. Betty took her place by a huge stone alter. Three dark figures with blue on were sitting above three other figures wearing red, they were sitting also. These six were facing Betty and six others on the other side of the alter. A huge fire burned at the foot of the platform where they sat. In front of the six red and blue cloaked was a bowl decorated in jewels, a goblet, and some sort of dagger. In the fire were 13 branding irons. On the alter was a man, naked and chained to the stone.

One blue cloaked figure rose up. Betty and the others went silent and kneeled. The figure was an Elder. He said in the Coven language, "Tonight we sacrifice thee to Menod Natsatis. We give impure blood to our Lord in exchange for purity. Many have left us and we have gained new. Now it is time to purify 82."

One of the red cloaked figures moved about, went to the fire and handed each of the black cloaked figures a branding iron. The Coven started chanting again, as if it wasn't them controlling what they were saying. It was memorized into their heads as to what to say and do. Betty felt like she was inside a television. It was as if she was given lines to rehearse and she had them scorched into her head. The man was obviously a bum from off the street. A nobody. One by one the figures in black blazed a symbol into the man, saying in the Coven language "Now shall I be pure." Betty's symbol looked like a rose. The man screamed in fright as they each burned a symbol onto his naked smelly body.

Then another elder said, "We have three new witches amongst us. Step up to the altar."

Instantly Betty felt herself move up to the crying hobo. She was on automatic. Two others joined her at either side. They got up onto the altar in front of the homeless man. They bared their bodies in front of him. Betty, out of curiosity glanced slightly to see the other two cloaked bodies. They were male. As if being pushed by an unknown force, the three of them kneeled. Then chanted "Let us be purified!"

The three Highest and the three Elders took their branding irons and burned a symbol into the three black cloaked new witches. Betty didn't feel it. It was as if she was numb. The three of them raised their arms to their dark Lord and automatically began to chant. Their bodies exposed for all to see. The Highest took their daggers and sliced open the homeless man. Because Betty's head was bowed, there in the altar were grooves and the man's blood drained down into small silver cups which were filled already with a clear liquid. The blood swirled in a fascinating delight as it mixed into the other liquid. The fire light and blood reflected with a sheer splendor off the silver. The Elders ran their hands over the man and then over the new witch bodies in a purification. Two females; one dressed in a red cloak and the other dressed in a blue cloak, ran their hands over Betty's naked body. The blood was warm. The other hands were of men and she with the other two witches was saturated in blood. The others, who were dressed in black cloaks, took the cups and drank unto the dark Lord.

Ava couldn't listen to this anymore. The thought was sickening to her stomach. She turned towards the heavy door and walked out into the hospital hallway. Her hands over her mouth. She was swallowing the lump that rose from her throat.

"Ava!" Trent was coming after her. "She wants you in there." He said as he approached her.

"I don't want to hear it Trent!" Ava was thoroughly grossed out. "Lies, all lies. Betty is dying and all she can do is tell some horror story she made up!" Ava started to cry.

"I've heard of these Covens Ava." Trent said taking his wife's arm gently. Ava stopped in the busy hallway. Trent replied, "The one she is talking about may be real. Look at how many people have died mysteriously in Skull County."

"Then you go back and listen to it. I've had enough." Ava put her hands on her face to hide the crying. "I can't take it anymore."

"She won't tell me without you being there. I can't save her without a full confession. Please Ava, you don't want to see Betty fall into the pits of hell. She is your friend." Trent voice was soothing but to listen to the garbage from Betty's mouth was too much.

Ava looked into her husband's eyes. Soft bluish

green. Loving, compassionate. He wore a very concerned face. Slight wrinkles formed by his eyes from squinting in the sun and years of laughter. His slight trace of freckles across his nose. Ava turned and headed outside for fresh air.

"Ava?" Her husband followed her. "Please."

Ava sat down on a bench. "I really need to think about this. I love Betty but I can't take this blood and Coven bullshit you know."

"The dream she had," Trent said sitting next to her, his voice quiet, "she mentioned that you were in that dream she had. You were on the other side of the gate. Do you remember this?"

"She is always on the other side of a gate." Ava paused an uncomfortable pause. "Yes, I have that dream often. To this day I have this dream." Ava said crying.

"Then she isn't lying Ava. There is no way you can have the same dream unless it is real. We need to help her Ava." Trent was determined.

"Can I just have a moment Trent? Just a moment of silence. I really need to pray about this. I really need to pray." Ava just sat there crying and shaking. She wrapped her arms around herself and rocked back and forth in a comfort mode. Trent put his hand on her shoulder.

"I'll be in with Betty." He said. "I love you and I will pray also." Trent got up from her side with confusion but understanding Ava's uncomfortable situation. He walked back towards the hospital doors.

Ava sat there watching him walk away. She was tremendously scared of what Betty just told. She felt just as helpless as Betty but not so battered and bruised. Just bruised on the inside. Ava closed her eyes and held her tear streaked face towards the last rays of the sun. Dusk came so early this evening. Even though it was spring, it felt like winter all over again. A chilled wind blew from the north. Icy and cold. Ava decided to return even though she didn't want to hear about it. Betty needed her right now. A good friend.

SUMMER SCHOOL

Summer of 1993. Betty finally moved out of her father's house and in a small camping trailer with some friends. Summer school had just started. Ava was taking photography and math courses so that she could pass her senior year a bit more quickly. Betty had the same photography course but also had two other courses to take in order to pass her junior year. Betty was behind from all that ditching. It was now that Ava and Betty could spend a little time together like old pals without anyone noticing the preppy and the stoner talking about the real life.

Betty actually got to photography classes on time. Even though it was the beginning of the course, she did show up 15 minutes early. Unusual. She even looked good, no bruises, and a genuine smile as she entered the classroom.

"Good morning Ava." Betty said as she tossed her book bag over the chair and onto the table top.

"Hi Betty. Wow, you are in a good mood." Ava smiled back. "What's the occasion?"

"Ah life is great to me." Betty told her as she took the seat next to her. "I'm partially on my own, I have a job, I'm getting a car, and I have a new boyfriend."

Betty was on cloud nine.

"Oh, so that is the secret. A new man." Ava rolled her eyes in a good way. "Who is he? Do I know him?"

"Nope." Betty smiled ear to ear. "He's an out of towny from the bay area." With that, she reached into her bag and took out a picture. The picture was from some photo booth that you'd see on a boardwalk or at a fair. Those small silver booths that you feed your money into, draw back the curtain, and cram all your friends in. This new out of towny guy was cute. Too bad it was in black and white. A row of six pictures of Betty and a man smiling, kissing, and being silly. "Isn't he just the hottest?" She said with a sigh.

"A little young isn't he?" Ava said with a curious smile.

"He's 18 with side burns Ava..." Betty's little piece happiness disappeared.

"Oh, yes I see now. The peach fuzz is a dead giveaway." Ava laughed. "I was being sarcastic Betty, laugh with me."

"Sorry." Betty said with a straight and narrow look. "You get so serious and then I don't catch the sarcasm. You need to smile while saying the joke Ava or someone will knock your teeth down your throat for being that way."

"No they won't you dork!" Ava was laughing hard. "You just pulled serious sarcasm right there."

"I'm serious, that wasn't funny." Betty was then laughing with Ava anyway because it didn't sound so serious after all.

Ava was feeling like it was old times again with Betty. She felt good that Betty didn't completely shut her out. They were laughing, talking, and being best friends again. The catch was in Ava's mind; how long will it last this way? Until the end of summer? In Ava's heart, she was hoping it wouldn't end.

Class started up and out the door 30 students went with a camera in hand from the journalism room on the lower campus of Skull High. Betty and Ava walked up towards the graveyard with a few other fellow students. The teacher, Mr. Stevens, was like a watch dog. One minute there would be silence and not a soul around. The next thing you know, he is at the corner and lurking in the summer shade. Oddly shaped tall man with bleached out hair. Wonder if he dyed it blond. It looked so un-natural the way it just flopped on his head as he bobbled about watching students. Wig? It could've been a wig.

Up in the graveyard there wasn't much to take pictures of. Betty would lay on the graves jokingly playing dead as Ava took pictures of her. Or it would be vice versa. There was nothing on campus to take pictures of since the school had the lockers ripped out. Betty thought of taking the camera home so that she could get assignments done. Ava had agreed. There were plenty of pictures to be taken at home.

"We could get together this weekend and set up a studio in my parent's garage." Ava said to Betty.

"That would be kick ass. I still don't understand about this shadowing part of photography. Did you do that assignment yet?" Betty was winding up film on a reel in the dark room. Ava was sitting with her. "I did the pinhole assignments and the negative press assignments but not the shadowing. I don't want to take pictures of some damn egg." Betty giggled.

"I was thinking." Ava said. "Instead of an egg, let's do fruit or even people's faces."

Betty snapped the reel into its metal dispenser and put the lid on. Her hands were starting to sweat in the little black bag. "Don't they have AC in this old classroom? I'm sweating to death. It feels like furnace in this place."

Ava replied, "And?"

"Oh," Betty said as she took out her hands from the bag and took out the metal container. "yeah I guess. Whose face are we going to use for shadowing?"

"We could use my dad." Ava started to laugh. Her father was an old hippie from the sixties and his face was worn with age. Wrinkles and lines everywhere from stress, laughter, and sun. His hair gray and grisly, long and put back into a ponytail. Nice old man.

"Well," Betty laughed with her. "It is better than fruit."

"You can have dinner at my house Friday evening. We could meet after summer school." Ava commanded, just like a prep director.

"Sure, only one problem." Betty said as the two of them started out the dark room door. "I can't stay the night."

"Just dinner. I know you have plans." Ava smiled.

"Yep." Betty smiled back. Her eyes twinkled a glimmer of silver.

After school everyone either got onto the buses provided or stayed to go swimming at the high school pool. Some of the stoners would be out on the football field smoking cigarettes or at a little restaurant called The Patio for french fries and shakes. Ava had tennis lessons down at the courts by the football field. She would watch Betty hang around with her stoner friends. A part of Ava wished for the carefree life of Betty. But, the other part of Ava knew it meant trouble down the long haul.

Betty; tall and average looking. Long black wavy hair always worn down. Full figured hips, small breasts that were pushed up by a padded bra. Medium structure for her size. Her eyes that were dark brown never shimmered a silver hue before. Ava found that a bit odd. Betty's popularity was quite strange as well. May be her being kicked out of school had something to do with that. Betty was different somehow. Ava grew curious.

"Ava!" Her tennis instructor shouted. "Pay attention will yeah!" Her instructor was a tiny old woman who wore miniskirts and little pom pom ankle socks. "You have plenty of time to play after we practice."

"Heck I don't play anymore." Ava laughed. "I was just curious about my friend over there."

The old lady batted the ball over the net into Ava's court. Again Ava missed the green felt ball and it hit the fence behind her. The instructor looked over at the stoners. "The raven haired one? She is trouble." She put her hands on her hips and stared. "Oh yeah, she is definitely not worth playing with." Then the instructor got back into a stance position to retrieve the ball.

Ava hit the ball back to the old lady. "Why do you say that?"

The instructor hit the ball to Ava in hopes that she would return it to her. "Well for one, I can see she is into something dark. It is as plain as day!"

Ava finally hit the ball but the ball flew out of lines and off onto the side. "No not Betty?" She said in disbelief.

The instructor reached for a used ball that was sitting by her feet. "That girl is vile. If you can't see the black cloud well," the instructor served the next ball to Ava, "you are sure blind as a Christian."

"Ha!" Ava smirked as she gave it her all and hit the ball as hard as she could, "screw you old woman!" The tennis ball flew nice and high over the net and into the ladies court space.

"Oh yeah," the instructor laughed, "use your anger, nice hit Ava!" The play went on for about eight hit counts and then Ava lost again.

"So, tomorrow after summer school Ava?" the instructor said with a gleam of defeat in her eye.

"As always." Ava pouted as she took a large drink of water from her water bottle. "So," she asked the instructor, "you really think Betty is evil?"

The instructor was loading up her equipment into a large duffle bag. "Yes and I am warning you young lady, stay far away from that girl. You'll get sucked into something you will wish you'd never seen. Evil lurks there." she gave Betty who was sitting on her boyfriend a long hard stare. "Evil." she reminded Ava again.

The next day at summer school Ava had to ask Betty questions. Betty was pretty much a tight box to open. "Betty," Ava started in, "what do you do on Fridays?"

"I go to Allen's house and hang out." Betty said bluntly.

"What do you do during the weekdays?" Ava asked.

"Well," Betty said, "I hang out around here with my boyfriend until about 6 or so, go home and do my studies, drink a few beers, make dinner and watch television."

"You drink beer?" Ava gasped. "You can't buy beer!"

"Yes I can and I do." Betty smiled.

"What? Fake ID? An older friend?" Ava asked in curiosity.

"I know where you are going with this Ava." Betty was now looking straight into Ava's eyes. "The old bat is wrong. She has not a clue."

"Betty." Ava was now whispering. "That was creepy. What the hell? Have you been listening to my tennis instructor and I's conversation?"

"That is your instructor? Oh man she is a freak!" Betty started laughing. "She is like how old wearing pink tutu's and prancing around those courts like she is a five year old! Damn though, she has some awesome legs!"

"You eavesdropped," Ava was raged, "you bitch!"

"Nope I didn't do that." Betty stopped laughing and got real serious.

"Then what the hell? How can you possibly know what we talked about then?" Ava was starting to get snotty.

"Look Ava." Betty's eyes turned that strange hue of silver. "I know what you are thinking deep down inside that pretty little mind of yours. I know you've never kissed a man, you are still a virgin, and that you are curious to know about certain things about me." Betty got quiet, her voice shifted in tone. "Someday I will take you." Then the whole mood in the air changed as quickly as it had shifted. "But not today." Betty said in a now friendly tone.

"Are you spying on me?" Ava didn't get it. She

was in denial about what just happened.

"Ava, drop it." Betty said with and with a few unknown words Ava forgot what she was trying to do.

Friday approached and after school as Betty promised, met Ava and they took off uptown towards Main Street. Ava's father was to meet them in Black Bart Park by the hotel. Betty was dressed in blue jeans and a black tank top. Her hair was now actually up in a ponytail. She looked nice with her hair up off her face.

"Do you have a camera?" Ava asked Betty.

"The damn teacher wouldn't let me sign one out so I had to snag it." Betty said with a grumpy voice. "I'll return it on Monday."

"I don't think too many adult figures trust you. I think it is the crowd you hang out with." Ava said in a sympathetic tone.

"Its bullshit how they all treat me." Betty was upset. "It doesn’t matter if I am nice, mean, or even kissing ass, they will always hate me and distrust me."

"It's a small town and a small school." Ava said honestly. "The only thing they know is that you are a rebel against your father and they all hate the man. It may be their way of getting even with him."

"Yeah well, they don't have to use me to get to him." Betty said. "I don't even live with the bastard anymore."

"No but you are his blood." Ava said.

"No I'm not!" Betty shouted. The two girls were laying in the coolness of the lawn. Betty jumped up and started to walk to the drinking fountain.

In the smallest of the warm summer breeze, Ava heard a familiar voice say "Reziah". It carried through the slight wind and Betty lifted her head from the water fountain.

"What was that Betty?" Ava was trying to remember where she heard that voice. "Did you hear that?"

"Hear what?" Betty put her head down and took another sip of water ignoring what she did hear.

"Raziah." Ava repeated. "What does that mean?"

"I don't know? Are you going paranoid on me?" Betty started to giggle. "Ava," She said, "you are losing it my dear."

"What ever." Ava laughed and she tucked this into the back of her mind for later.

Ava's father was rather late to pick up the girls from the park. They had already taken a few pictures around Main Street. When they got to the house, Ava set up a crude studio in the garage and her father poised for the two girls. Then they went out into the neighborhood and took pictures of mailboxes and nature. Dinner was at seven in the evening. Betty hadn't eaten a square meal since she had left home so for her it was a treat. She had been living on macaroni and cheese, hamburger helper, and twinkies. Ava's mom made steamed green beans fresh from the garden with bacon pieces, fried chicken, fruit jello, and steamed white rice.

"You don't have to go back Betty." Ava said after her mom took the empty dinner plates off the table. "Dad and I discussed it and you could stay here."

"Ava I can't." Betty told her with a slight sadness. "I have a place now and I really want to do this on my own."

"Well," Ava looked down at her hands that were placed on the empty spot where her plate once had been, she looked up at Betty, "you are always welcome here okay." Ava's heart sank. She felt something wrong with Betty.

"Thank you Ava. I'll remember that." Betty said with honesty. "I should get going. I have a long day tomorrow."

Betty stayed until 9 in the evening. She was pushing it. Deep down, she didn't want to go to her shared trailer. She didn't want to go to the Coven meeting. She wanted out. She was free from her father now and didn't need magic anymore. Her life was now how she wanted it to be. She felt, trapped.

She and Ava talked about the good old past when they were young and full of energy. The shared memories of who had the most dolls, when they had tea parties under the shade tree in Ava's yard, and when it was raining how they dressed in Ava's mothers clothes. The two girls ended up crying together at the dinner table before Betty left. They were such innocent memories. Memories held so dear in Betty's heart.

When she got to her place of living, her roommate was already asleep. Betty quietly opened the door and lit a candle. She began to rethink her life. In three hours a black car would drive up. Mister would drive her out into the wooded hills of Skull County and drop her off. Betty had already been to fifteen Coven meetings and the dreams were so intense now that she hadn't dreamed of anything else since she did that prayer. Her dreams are always the same. The same damn forest, the same pathways, the same huge wall that she has tried to climb over but can't, the fountain that spurts dark water, the brook that screams louder and louder now, the stone that a new comer stands on, the same faces that now take on different animal shapes when they are about to disappear, the tower with no windows or doors. It has become a nightmare.

Betty had already assassinated a few ex-coven people. She was assigned to kill them. The first person was easy. At the Coven meeting she was drawn out of a golden bowl, the Assassins Bowl. All new witches had to have their name in the bowl. They gave her instructions. A Mister came to pick her up. She did what was instructed and went home. Betty had to cut a car's wiring. Breaks? She didn't know and she didn't care. The second assassination was a lady in her own home. The lady had a child. Betty made it look like a suicide. She can still hear the small infant screaming for its mother in her head.

Betty shook the memory out of her mind. She held her face in her hands. She wanted out without being assassinated herself. She was in too deep now. With the Coven they had made a storm over a city, met other Covens around them, casting spells over people, drank blood, killed animals bigger than sheep, and even sacrificed humans. Betty started to sob. As she sat on her fold out trailer bed, she wrapped her arms around her legs and cried. The Mister would show up, she would undress, and tonight Coven 82 will begin a summer love spell. A casting that would pick who will be the next Hasbrath, the goddess of all creation. Menod Natsatis needs his Queen.

Chapter Four

When Betty stopped crying it was as if time had flown by. It was now 11 PM. She quietly pulled out a large shoe box that once held a pair of Doc Marten boots. In the box was her cloak, a jeweled dagger that she acquired through the Coven, her slipper shoes, and her book. She thumbed through the book looking for something to cover up her fear. The pages for the first time were blank. Nothing. Not one typed or even written word on any of the pages. Being a bit creeped out, she put the book back into the box and shoved the box deep under her fold out bed. Chills ran up her spine.

Betty grabbed her stuff with a pack of cigarettes and like a mouse went out the door into the summer night. Fresh air filled her lungs. She headed towards the road to wait. She was early this time. Too early. But, she waited anyway. She kept dwelling on what the Coven had done lately besides the Assassinations, killing of human and animals, and the drinking of strange blood. The magic was too intense, too real. Betty's once short hair was now incredibly long. Her eyes could change to any color she wished of. Her beauty once average was now becoming more noticeable. Her lack of faith in herself was now bold. She could hear people's thoughts as if they were talking directly to her. She could see the future just by glancing into a reflection. She could become any animal she wished and was able to eavesdrop on someone just by being their pet cat.

Betty sat out in the warm summer night thinking about the things she was able to do. She watched the glittering summer stars shining on a velvet dark blue sky. She was scared and had a feeling that someone might pick up on that at the Coven. "Come on Betty." She told herself. "Release it. Release the fear. Be the rock, the iron rock. Feel nothing." She whispered to the stillness of the night. Betty then started to chant a casting for herself of courage. She started to fall asleep.

The realm of other things started to suck her into the fleshiness. That dark hollow place before being spit into the meadow with tall grass that felt like long willowy fingers on her naked body. She tried to force herself awake but she sunk deep into the world of hell. She found herself in the dim meadow. Betty started to look around her. She knew she might not return to the other side where her sleeping body was. In panic she started to run into the woods. She felt the cold sweat dripping down her back and between her arms. She kept thinking that the others will smell her fear so she stopped at the huge tall stone wall at the edge of the forest.

Betty frantically looked about to see if anyone followed her or even heard her running, breathing, and gasping for air. Her eyes jetted about the dark shadows for figures. Nothing. She was alone. She then picked up again and started running towards the iron gate that closed up the forest. Her heart pounded in her head and chest. Out of breath she started yelling for Ava. She wrapped her fingers around the iron bars that kept her from the lush green lawn and sunlight. She gripped them so tight her fingers actually started to turn colors.

"AVA" she yelled. She waited for an answer. A long pause of silence. No one. Not one soul out there. Betty then started to shake the bars and scream manically. Tears rolled down her cheeks. She started to fight the iron bars of the gate for her freedom but instead the iron cut right through her skin of her hands. "No, no, no, no." She wept. "I have to get out. You can't keep me here; you can't keep me I'm not yours to take." She dropped to the ground and wrapped her arms around her legs. Naked, sweaty, and cold Betty rocked herself back and forth. "I need to wake up damn it. Wake up." She told herself out loud.

Finally a horn went off. Betty jerked up and noticed she was back. The Mister stared at her. He honked the horn again. Betty got up from where she was sitting and picked up her stuff slowly with stiffness. She hated the feeling of going in through that hell, that dark fleshy womb of hell. She got into the black car and gave The Mister an evil grin. "What's your problem?" she said to him.

The Mister went from staring at her through the rear view mirror then quickly to the road ahead. "You want out." The Mister has never talked to her before, ever. His voice was mono tone. There was absolute no feeling or emotion to the voice.

"Screw you and drive." Betty said covering up her true feelings with anger.

"I can help you." The Mister said. "No one will ever know." He sounded like one of those old films that you load in a movie projector. A hypnotic tone. One note. Very low. Robotic. Mechanical.

Betty just ignored him. He said nothing more after that. She got dressed and stuffed her clothing in the box. She smoked three cigarettes before she arrived. She flipped her hood over her head and practically jumped out of the car. She used her anger to hide her real feelings about what she was about to do. As usual, she followed the Coven into the cave that was out in the middle of Jesus Maria Road. The heaviness was intense inside. The air was hotter than the summer stillness.

The ritual lay in front of the black cloaked Coven members. It was a buck. Large with a rack of ten horns, five on either side. Beautiful creature with a smooth tawny coat of fur. It was sedated under a spell but its eyes were wide and huge as silver dollars staring right at Betty. The reflection in the buck's eyes, she could see a future. It was like ripples of sand moving across her vision. It started out as a big black dot with the fire reflecting back and flickering. She couldn't stop it from happening. Soon all the little sand particles took place as if a grainy picture or movie screen. Then it got real clear. With its force and power her body jerked and she was standing in it.

The future was of the day. An afternoon. She was inside a house. Ava's house. Betty didn't want to see this so she tried to close her eyes. Her eyes were already closed. Betty forced herself to wake up from this vision but her eyes were already open as well. So she reluctantly watched this future just to get it over with. Ava, there standing by the phone on the wall.

Talking about people. Who? About men.

"I don't know. I really like Trent but I kind of want to go out with Phil tonight." Ava said to someone on the phone. A pause. Then Ava answered back, "Really no way! Phil wouldn't do that." another pause. "Well I can't go out with him if he isn't going to respect me." another pause. Then she answered back to the person on the receiving end, "I just don't kiss on the first date."

There was more to the vision but Betty blacked out. The Elders were above her crumpled form and the three of them helped her up. "What a mighty vision you bring to us Reziah." An elder said. The tallest Elder.

The whole Coven chanted "Reziah is chosen." and the entire Coven helped her up towards the sacrificial deer that was chained to the stone alter.

"Who else shall be chosen to bring forth Hasbrath?" The lady Elder said in the Coven language.

The Coven members chanted a member of the Highest. A Priestess. Then they chanted another member in black. Betty kneeled in front of the huge beast on one side of the Highest and the other girl kneeled by the Highest also. The three of them were kneeling. All three girls whipped back their cloaks so that the others could see their naked bodies but not their faces. The Coven started to chant the casting to bring forth Menod Natsatis. The Elders poured some sort of black liquid into three large silver chalices decorated in stones. Then they handed these to the three of them. Each with their own cup. They raised the chalices to "Their Lord" and drank.

The chanting started to sound erotically musical. Betty's head was spinning in a good way. She started to feel loosened up. She drank the entire cupful of blackness. Thick, warm, sweet blackness. The cup fell to the floor from her hands. Her hands felt piloted automatically and she started to rub herself. Over her breasts, her hardened nipples, her hips. She glanced in the direction of the other two girls kneeling beside this inviting creature. They too were rubbing themselves. The Highest had her fingers inside herself and she was moaning. Betty joined her; they were rubbing and fingering each other. Betty felt the animal stir. The third girl was joining them, rubbing, fingering, and licking. The animal moved again.

With this, Betty started rubbing the huge buck. Her fingers went over the smooth course fur. Then she was noticing that her fingers were one with the animal. She felt the animal's blood. It ran hot and sensual through its veins. She then ran her hand over its belly and towards its groin. Her hand melted right into the animal. Somehow out of nowhere three nice sized manly shafts came out between the buck's legs. The buck was no longer a deer shape but a man with legs like a deer and hooves. He had three hard ready shafts. They were positioned perfectly for the three girls to ride on and get pleasure out of. Betty was astonished and hot with need to fulfill herself. The ache for sex was incredibly sky rocketing.

The three girls were melting in and out of this strange creature as if they were all one.

When Betty was wet with excitement she stuck the creature's shaft into her. It moved and it made her feel full. She didn't have to move herself around to get pleasure, it pleasured her by sinking into her flesh and twisting, whirling, and going in and out rapidly - slowly and rapidly again. The Highest was in the middle, sandwiched between the two black cloaked ones. Betty and the other black cloaked witch were caressing The Highest. Sucking on her nipples, biting, teasing, and licking.

The three witches were melting into each other. They were one with the creature. Oh how Betty wanted to kiss The Highest but it would be against protocol. So instead, Betty started to kiss the manly creature she was riding. His tongue entered her mouth, it was wet and all about the erotic playful lick. She licked his lips and he licked the upper roof of her mouth. She sucked on his tongue, flicking it with hers and he sucked on her lower lip, gently biting it.

This strange orgy must have gone on until dawn. The whole Coven was having sex with one another without showing their heads. The cave smelled strongly of pheromones. Betty noticed that she was not seeing through her eyes but the other two girls and the creature's eyes. It was intense. She could hear their thoughts and feel what they were feeling. She had sex in the realm but it was nothing ever so extreme like this. She loved it. She watched the others as they were all naked baring their bodies to this sexual delight.

She noticed that they were all covered in blood. They were rubbing each other in it. Kissing each other's bodies. Sucking on the men's shafts. Fingering and licking the girl witches crotches. The dirt floor was turning into mud. Dark red mud. Where was the blood coming from? Betty watched a few girl witches get pumped by the men in a dog style position. As those girl witches were getting it hard and fast, they dug into the ground with their hands and one grabbed her ass as if for more. Another's face was buried into the mud. They were all covered in bloody mud.

As soon as daylight peaked slightly above the hill top, spontaneously they all reached a peak of orgasm. Coven 82 stopped what they were doing and they chanted one last chant to "Their Lord" in praise. Then they filed out of the cave and towards the creek and over the rickety bridge. One by one they disappeared into the scattered oak trees. Betty; tired and feeling really strange found The Mister who waited for her. She hopped into the car. She realized she was covered in blood as well. How could this be when she was not rolling in it with the rest of them? Blood was starting to crust on her skin and itch. She wiped herself off as much as she could and got dressed. Her womanly parts felt sore from all night's worth of sex. Lazily she lit up a cigarette.

Betty didn't dare fall asleep. She was afraid to. When the dawn of morning finally filled the powder blue sky with peach hues, The Mister dropped her off at the road side where Betty lived. She watched him drive off down the road around the bend. Where does The Mister go afterwards? Was he and the other Misters a part of another Coven? Betty hurried towards the dumpy little camper trailer. She wanted a shower in the worst way. Her whole body ached everywhere. Tired and sore. She entered the trailer noisily. Her roommate woke up, looked at her, and then flopped her head back down on her pillows. She didn't say anything.

Betty grabbed out her box and put her Coven things into it. She shoved it deep under her fold out bed. Then she walked towards the back where the small bathroom was located. She stripped off her clothing, turned on the water, and hopped on in. The hot water was soothing. The crusted blood on her skin soaked up the water and started to swirl its way like miniature rivers down her body to the drain. Betty took the white bar of soap and started to scrub herself. She dared not use a wash cloth. In the bathroom there was no shower curtain. It was an open shower that got everything wet except for your clothing and towels which were tucked into a cubby hole and protected by a small hinged door.

While Betty scrubbed off the blood from her aching body, she also had to wipe off splatters of blood on the walls, ceiling, and counter with her hands. In order for her not to get so wigged out about it, she pretended it was hair dye. She ended up shaving her legs, her armpits and she shaved her pubic hair into a nice shapely V. She scrubbed her head and took a toothbrush to her face. Time must have slipped by; Betty was in the shower for an hour and forty five minutes. She dried herself off with a towel that was poked away in the cubby hole. She dronishly stepped out of the tiny bathroom with a towel wrapped around her and headed to her bed.

Chapter Five

Her roommate must have been angry because as soon as Betty sat on her bed, the roommate shot a dirty look at her and slammed the bathroom door behind her. Wonder how long she'd been waiting to use the bathroom? Betty was so dog tired that she fell asleep with the towel around her. That sinking feeling came on quickly. She was soon sucked into the fleshy doorway of hell and spit out into the damn meadow again. All the Covens were there, and they were all bowed down before Menod Natsatis. Betty joined in reluctantly and bowed along with the others. All 85 Covens were there chanting to their Lord. They circled him in the meadow. He was in the center of them. Standing there naked.

Menod Natsatis gave a speech when the Covens ended the chant. His speech was about his match, his Queen. He had one female picked out of 31 females. Mathematically speaking there are four types of females and one of them is exactly what he sought out. 54 people out of the 85 Covens were either male or another kind of female which he did not want. 85 equals 13 and 13 equals the four houses, four females. In a way, Betty felt a sudden respect for that. But on the other hand, she feared it too.

Menod Natsatis went on about the chosen female and how he would announce it during the Harvest. The 31 females were called by their coven names to kneel in front of him. Betty took her place by Layla and kneeled. Layla glanced Betty's direction with a vicious smile. Betty felt her thought like a razor cutting through her mind. "I will be the chosen one and you will die Betty." With that thought, Betty twitched a little. Menod Natsatis must of seen Betty shiver because she could see his bare perfect feet in front of her now.

"Reziah." He said. The Covens repeated her name. "Reziah, why so frightened like a bird?"

"I fear you my Lord." she replied. "I fear your power over human creation."

"I love your fear. I smell it." His voice was seductive. "It is good to fear me and you are an example for the others to see. I want them to fear me, love me, want me, and desire me."

The Coven was now humming a low sound as they bowed before Menod Natsatis. Betty was sweating like a leaky faucet. She had not a clue what he could do to her. She gripped the fleshy grass before his feet. "Please my Lord," she started to beg, "do not hurt me."

"Reziah." Menod Natsatis said as he touched her

shoulder. His fingers were soft, his hand was pale. His skin was flawless. "You are my example of fear." and with that he turned her into a bird in front of the entire Coven. "When you fear no more you will require your human shape here again."

Betty was now small and fragile. In fear, she flew off into the woods. There were no creatures in the forest accept for a small few. They never lasted long. Always disappearing and never seen again. Betty flew over the forest towards the wall. Her little wings wouldn't allow her to go over the wall like she wanted. The wall was much too high. But maybe she could squeeze through the iron gate bars now being such a tiny fearful size. She started to fly over to the gate but the realm, like a straw, sucked her out and back to where she was laying on her bed at home.

Betty opened her eyes and just stared at the stained ceiling above her. For a moment she had not a clue where she was. She just stared off into that space trying to remember. When recollection past, she then tried to remember what she had a dream of. What was it that made her feel frightened? Why was it so dark in this trailer? Betty peeled herself into an upright position and looked at the red glowing digital alarm clock.

"Shit!" She exclaimed. "nine o'clock?" She was

confused about that.

She took the towel off and dug around for some clothing. She had so much to do. Grocery shopping, homework, and a party to attend at Layla's house. The day was wasted on sleep. Sleep. Betty paused in realization. She finally was able to sleep. Or did she? She can't remember if she was there in her sleep or not. Her head felt empty instead of full. Shaking her head like shaking it off, she began to put on clothes. She took a look around the trailer for her roommate. The roommate was gone. Everyone must be at the party already and probably has been there since six this evening.

Betty hurried out the door and locked it. The evening air felt good in her lungs. She hadn't had a cigarette for about 16 hours now. Talking to herself, "May be now is time to quit." But when she reached into her flannel pocket she could feel a pack of Marlboro's. "Nah." She giggled and took out a smoke to light up. She headed towards the road that winds around and over a seasonal creek. The sun had settled and the stars of twilight twinkled brightly over the country back roads. When she finally reached Pool Station Road she noticed that it was quiet. Usually you could hear Layla's parties right at her gate. Her parent's house was up on the hill that over looked the drab town of St. Andrew.

Betty opened the green heavy gate and started a steady walk up the dirt drive way. When she got to the first flat and the house was visible, she seen that most of the lights were on and that the garage door was opened. She stopped to catch her breath and lit up another cigarette. Then she headed towards the smaller incline of the hill. She walked stealthy over the cattle guard and walked up to the quiet house. Too quiet for Betty's liking. It was spooky. Betty went inside the bright garage to the door. She stared at the gold door knob. It started to turn. Right as she looked up to see who it was, Allen came into the garage from out of nowhere.

The door opened but Betty's attention was on Allen. "Hey Betty what's up?" Layla said noticing that Allen was standing in the opening of the two door garage.

Betty didn't even look at Layla but she answered her back. "It's so freak'n quiet around here. Not like the usual parties is it?"

"No," Layla smiled. "Just a few friends this time."

Betty turned to Layla and sheepishly smiled.

"Betty." Layla said with a strange absurd tone. "You are late."

"I was sleeping. Was up all night." Betty answered back. "Can I come in?"

Allen finally approached the two of them. He was acting unusual. "Let her in Layla." He broke the silence.

"Of course!" Layla finally laughed. Though it made Betty uncomfortable.

Inside the house sitting in the living room were some new faces. Layla introduced two new men to Betty and a girl who was loud and obnoxious. She was named Chance. Unusual for a girl's name. Then there was Allen, Grunt, and Dawson. Dawson was charming but far from being a partier. They were drinking Kailua and watching television. Layla sat down on the floor and laid out on a bean bag. Allen joined her but like a cat that had enough maleness, she shoved Allen off her bean bag and she laughed at him. Dawson decided to sit and lay next to Layla and she didn't budge. Allen then sat next to Betty who was on the other side of the living room away from Layla.

"Betty." Allen smiled sweetly. "How come you couldn't sleep last night?" his question to this had seemed sincere.

"Wouldn't you like to know?" Betty smiled back. He did know. Everyone in the Coven must have slept all day. Didn't they?

"Layla is such a bitch." Allen blurted in a whisper to Betty.

"You're just saying that because you are phishing for information Allen." Betty smiled at him. He was sitting a bit too close for her comfort. Grunt was sitting in a huge over sized chair observing everyone but had to giggle at the scene of Betty and Allen.

"No I mean it. I think she put a hex on me." He laughed out loud. Everyone in the room turned and shooshed him to be quiet except for Layla. Grunt just smirked and drank his sickly sweet drink.

"If she did I don't see it." Betty told him quietly. "What are we watching anyway?" She asked.

Allen placed his warm hand on Betty's bare leg. She had worn shorts for the first time this summer. "Not sure and I don't care." His hand slipped between her thighs to the cuff of her black shorts.

Out of nervousness Betty asked the crowd, "What are we watching?" and she scooted herself to the arm of the couch away from Allen's reach. Again Grunt giggled at the scene of Betty and Allen.

Dawson looked up from the bean bag and told her, "Twin Peaks Fire Walks with Me"

Then Chance blurted out, "Teresa Banks and the Last Seven Days of Laura Palmer." Chance was sitting in between the two new men, her legs thrown over one guys lap and her head on the other. She was flirtatious.

"How much of this did I miss?" Betty asked the crowd.

"Not much, it just started." Grunt said with his eyes now fixed on the television screen.

Betty decided to move over to the bean bag and Allen followed. He was like a lost dog without a master since Layla was being mean to him. Betty finally let in to his rubbing her thighs even though she'd have liked to bit him in the arm. It was turning her on. His fingertips were like feathers against her clean skin. Soft and gentle. Betty wondered just how much he watched at the Coven last night. She wanted to ask questions about where the blood came from and exactly what he had seen. Instead she let the irrelevant movie take over her thoughts. The more she got involved with the movie; she realized just how much the movie was like their lives. Especially Layla's.

FRIENDSHIP

When the movie was over, the eight of them went upstairs to Layla's room. Layla broke out with an unusual Ouija ball. "I got this down in San Francisco." She said and they all closed in around it. The Ouija alphabet went around the highly polished ball from A to Z. The numbers went across being broken up by the M and N and the A and Z in the alphabet. The four seasons were printed in the corners of the numbers and letters on the bottom and a yes, no, a symbol for sunshine and a symbol of the moon on the top corners divided by the letters and numbers. There was a small "goodbye" written by the symbol of the moon and a strange drawing of an eye by the symbol of the sun.

The ball was set on a quartz crystal shaped dish to roll smoothly when asked a question and the planchette was like a little heart shaped crystal table with a key hole for viewing next to the point. It had three small wooden legs and it sat perfectly over the ball. The eight of them put their fingertips on the planchette. Layla looked around the group and smiled, she was about to say something.

Dawson blurted out, "This stuff isn't real."

"We aren't the ones moving the planchette around the ball Dawson. The ball moves itself." Chance said.

"Okay." Layla finally said with a fixed smile on her face. "Let us summon up something dead."

One of the guys from this little group whispered, "Is there someone dead among us?"

Magically the ball started to spin from the strange eye symbol to the word "yes". Then it revolved in its crystal dish back to the eye. Dawson started to turn a bit pale in the face. All fingers where on the planchette and no one touched the ball to make it spin.

Chance then asked the Ouija "Who is among us tonight?"

The ball seem to float in the crystal dish to certain letters which spelled out M A R Y.

Dawson in disbelief asked "Mary who?"

The ball then spelled out M A G D E and then froze. It went back to the eye. The eye drawing seem to be a retreat for the planchette key hole view. It was to tell the group that it was done answering until the next question.

Layla asked, "Who in this room do you not like Mary Magde?"

The magical spinning took place and spelled out,

"C H A N C E".

The entire group looked at the obnoxious blond and laughed. Chance laughing nervously asked "Why me?"

The ball then rolled around in its dish and spelled out in an answer, "Y O U (retreating to the eye) A R E (retreating to the eye) F A K E (retreating to the eye)" With this everyone started to laugh except for Chance.

Chance then asked, "Then who in this room is doing evil and is not fake?"

The ball spelled it out as plain as daylight. It spelled out Layla, Grunt and Allen's name. They smiled and laughed. It didn't spell out Betty's name.

Betty asked the Ouija a question. "I'm not evil?"

The ball spun around and spelled out "You are a bird."

Dawson laughed so hard that he snorted. "See this thing is so artificial. Betty is as human as me and yet this piece of wooden and glass crap says she is a bird."

Layla looked around. Then she asked it a question disregarding Dawson. "Who are you really?"

The ball spun around revolving to the letters "H A S B R A T H".

Grunt's eyes got real big and Allen just about

fainted. Layla and Betty just looked at each other in amazement. The others of course had not a clue who Hasbrath was. Without being questioned the ball started to spin uncontrollably and spelled out Layla's name over and over again. The palchette was trembling under their fingertips. The crystal felt burning hot. The two guys immediately took their fingers off the planchette. Dawson was laughing as if it were all a joke. The planchette flung across Layla's bedroom and stuck into a wall like a deadly weapon. Dawson then went silent and jumped up from his sitting position.

"That was some cool shit!" Chance said out loud. "I don't think this Ouija likes you Layla." and she started to laugh.

Dawson didn't say anything. He just stood there as if he seen a ghost. The other two guys started to laugh with Chance. Layla just stood there as silent as Dawson. Her face went pale. Allen tried to touch Layla on the shoulder but Layla shot him a dirty look and Allen dropped his hand back to his side.

"Well, Hasbrath has a mission for you Layla." Grunt smiled. "You are of the highest order. This didn't amaze me. You'll be picked for the harvest for sure now." No one but Allen, Layla, and Betty knew what Grunt was talking about. It just sounded like gibberish nonsense. For the first time, Betty saw fear in Layla. It was slight but it was a fear.

Layla got up and started to laugh with the crowd and pulled out the planchette from the wall. "Good thing Dawson wasn't sitting there." She said looking at Dawson who almost tinkled his pants in urine.

Dawson left the room out of embarrassment or in anger. No one knew why he left for certain. Probably to go outside to smoke. Betty hopped up onto Layla's cloud fluff bed and laid down. Allen snuggled by her side. Layla put her toy away and headed down to find Dawson. Chance, Grunt, and the other two guys sprawled out on Layla's floor. It was late and they all felt a bit sleepy after drinking, watching a movie and playing on the Ouija. With the bedroom lights dimmed, Chance started to make out with one of the guys. Feeling the stir of sexual arousal, Allen started to make out with Betty on Layla's fluffy bed. Grunt fell fast asleep half under the bed and half hanging out of the bed skirting.

There on Layla's bed, Betty and Allen had sex. It had started with a few simple touches and passionate kissing. Betty knew it was a revenge thing on Layla in Allen's eyes. But for Betty, it was because she really did have feelings for Allen. Betty didn't want to have anything to do with him due to Layla flirting with him. She didn't want to betray a friend. Although having sex on her friends bed was betrayal in itself. No one knew except for Allen and he was not the kiss and tell type. Or was he? Betty had to keep her guard up now around Layla just in case someone had a jealous streak.

Early in the morning, Betty crawled quietly out of Layla's bed. Trying not to step on Grunt or the others, she headed towards the door. She padded her way down the long stairwell and looked around for Layla. Dawson was asleep on the couch Betty sat on last night. Layla wasn't around. Betty headed for the door and went outside. She walked down the dirt driveway, through the gate and headed off to her home. She would have stayed another night but she was feeling a bit uncomfortable. Thoughts entered her mind about what the Ouija had mentioned. Her being a bird. Of course she didn't dream last night either and that bothered her. She always had a dream of some sort.

She walked uptown instead of taking back roads and found Layla's parents car outside the doughnut shop. Betty, out of curiosity, peeked through the window. She didn't see Layla's parents. She had seen Layla eating a pastry and drinking coffee. Layla didn't have her license to drive? Betty went inside and sat down in a chair opposite of Layla.

"Want a doughnut?" Layla asked.

"No but a cup of coffee sounds good." Betty smiled a bit uneasy.

"No doughnut?" Layla said stuffing the last of a chocolate éclair into her mouth.

"Layla you are funny." Betty giggled.

Layla waved her empty cup at the kid behind the counter for another cup. The cute little blond blue eyed must be gay. He rolled his eyes in a feminine manner.

"Come on please for me Travis." Layla smiled at him.

"Here have an extra cup damn it." He giggled a gay laugh and handed Betty a cup. Betty took Layla and her cup to the coffee perker and filled two cups with rich over roasted coffee. Dark and steaming. Probably been brewed hours ago because the scent was a little potent.

"Thanks Betty Cat." Layla said as Betty came back to the table with the coffee.

Layla started to load her coffee with sugar packets and little liquid creamers. "So what brings you to walk home so soon?"

"You probably already know why." Betty said with honesty in her eyes.

Layla looked into Betty's eyes. Then she laughed. "I am so sorry. Actually no I have not a clue as to what you feel guilty about." Layla then took a sip of her coffee.

"You don't know." Betty was confused. Here in front of her was supposed to be the all time mind reader witch, The Highest, the soon to be Queen Hasbrath and she has not a clue. Something was amiss.

"I had sex with Allen." Betty said with a puzzled look on her face.

"That doesn't surprise me." The kid at the counter blurted out. "Sorry for eavesdropping. I'll go clean the back of the shop." He smiled and left.

Layla didn't even flinch. She just took another sip of her coffee. For a while there was some awkward silence for Betty. She felt heat rise from her body as if she did something wrong. Her hands started to fumble and wrench. Her palms were sweating.

Then Layla smiled. "Well now he'll leave me alone. He is so clingy and irritating at times. I mean," she took another sip of her coffee and crossed her legs in her chair, "I love him as a friend but damn I don't want a boyfriend right now. I'm 17 years old and I run off often. Every time I run away he never comes with me on adventures."

Betty felt relieved. Her heart stopped pounding in her throat and her body heat went down. "So you are cool with this?" Betty asked.

"Look," Layla said with a stern eye, "I love him so much but I can't give him what he needs right now. Just be good to him if that is where it is going with you two. If he gets his heart broken by you, I'll hunt you down." Then she smiled at Betty. "You know I'll always be your friend. I'm as much scared of you as you are of me." Layla got up and snuck around the counter. "Doughnut? Cookie?"

"Um," Betty laughed. "You are so crazy Layla."

"I'm starving." Layla grabbed a few cookies, a chocolate cake doughnut and a bear claw. Then in a joking cute voice she said, "Come to the dark side we have cookies." and then she handed Betty a cookie. Freshly baked and still warm. A chocolate chip cookie. Layla smiled as she took her seat and crossed her legs again, "I'll give Travis money for this later when he comes out of the back."

"Thanks Layla," Betty smiled with release of the pressure of holding that secret in, "You are so cool." Betty and Layla ate their goodies and drank their coffee. Travis came back out and shook his head. He didn't say much; obviously this was Layla's hang out when she wanted to be alone. Travis must know a lot of things about Layla that others didn't know. Betty kept this in the back of her mind.

"You could come back up if you want to Betty. Chance can get annoying and I'd rather hang out with you." Layla said finishing her coffee which was more sugar than coffee.

"Alright." Betty said. "There is a part of me that likes Allen and then there is this part of me that wants to avoid him right now."

"I'll fix that." Layla told her. "I'll make it to where he isn't so clingy on you. I just don't want to be stuck with Chance all day long."

They smiled in agreement and left out the bakery door. Betty slid into the passenger seat of the car as Layla took the drivers position. "I wish my parents would let me have a license." Layla laughed. "But until then, they will just have to deal with me stealing their vehicles." She started up the thunderbird and a way they drove off down the street towards the home on the hilltop.

Layla had The Cure blasting in the warm morning air. It was a nice morning to take a cruise Betty thought. Somehow Layla picked up on that thought and went down Pool Station Road out towards the rock quarry. Betty then thought it would be a blast to go swimming being that it was Sunday in the summer and no one was working out at the quarry. Layla again picked up on the thought of Betty's.

"Swimming, it does sound like fun." Layla smiled.

They drove the slightly long winding road through the countryside to the rock quarry. Layla parked the car in front of the locked fence. Layla smirked, "I'll take care of that." and she popped the trunk.

The two girls got out of the car. Betty stood there in wonder. Layla went to the trunk and brought out a pair of heavy duty lock cutters. She then took the big chompers to the puny sized lock and snipped it. Betty laughed. Layla went back to the trunk and put the lock cutters away. Betty opened up the gates and then hopped back into the car. Layla drove up to the dock and parked again.

"Well, front row parking for a great day to swim." Layla laughed.

Betty jumped out of the car and stripped off her clothes. Layla followed behind her. The two girls went skinny dipping in the blue water of the quarry. They swam towards some cliffs and jumped into the water, laughed, swam, explored small caves and hiked naked around the place. They laid out in the warm sunshine.

Then they headed towards some buckeye trees so they wouldn't get sunburned. Layla made a nest of leaves to lay on. Betty copied the idea and they both fell asleep. Betty woke up here and there noticing that Layla was one minute screaming for help with her eyes wide opened as if she was awake and then sound asleep the next.

In concern, after the third time, Betty woke up her friend. "Layla, wow you had me worried for a moment. Are you okay?"

"I'm fine. Damn I was sleeping pretty hard." Layla said.

"Um no you were having nightmares." Betty told her.

"Really?" Layla was curious. "What do you mean? Was I twitching or something?"

Betty laughed. "No more like screaming for help."

"Very funny Betty." Layla said with a smile. "Nice joke."

Chapter Six

Betty didn't say anymore to Layla about her screaming in her sleep. Instead she laughed back as if it was a joke but noticed that something was going on much deeper than they both knew. The torment they were living in, here in reality and there in a dream. Betty didn't dream anymore though. It was if she was free from them now. She didn't even remember having the dreams of the "other side". The realm. Hell.

"We should swim back and dry off. Dawson and all them might be worried." Layla mentioned.

"Heck we should just hang out here and see if Allen and Grunt can't radar our location." Betty laughed as she got up from her little nest under the buckeye.

"They probably thrashed my parent's house in an anger rage." Layla said as she grabbed a low limb and pulled herself up. "I don't want them to light my house on fire." She laughed at her own words.

"I don't think they would go that far." Betty smiled. "But just in case, I'll race yeah to the other side." and she made a mad dash to the water and jumped in.

"You hippie!" Layla laughed and steadily came to

the water's edge to dive in. She dove into the cool refreshing water to swim after Betty. As her head surfaced for air Layla called out to Betty, "Your boobs were bouncing all over the place!"

"Layla," Betty was embarrassed, "you staring at my tits?"

"Heck I played with them the other night. Who can't stare after that?" Layla laughed trying to swim up to Betty.

"Layla I have a question for you." Betty said as she did a back float so that Layla could catch up.

"If it is 'are you bi' the answer is no. I'm just doing what the Coven wants me to do." Layla admitted.

"No silly that wasn't it." Betty laughed. Then she asked, "Where did all the blood come from?"

"You know," Layla said as she got to Betty's side in the water, "I don't know that answer. We'll have to ask one of the guys."

They swam up to the dock and climbed onto the wooden planks. Layla unbridled went to the car and popped the trunk. She came back with two towels. Betty dried herself off and slipped on her clothes. Layla took her time drying off as she was enjoying the brilliant sunshine. Betty deep down wished she could be like Layla. She had no fear about her body. She was gorgeous. Betty noticed that Layla shaved below very little and kept that part of herself trimmed. In Betty's eyes, Layla was a masterpiece that stepped out of the roaring 1920's.

Layla finally put on her clothes and took the towel from Betty. "I really don't want to go back you know." She smiled.

"And moments ago you wanted to go home." Betty laughed.

"I just feel so lazy." Layla said flopping on the hood of the car still naked.

"It's the sun and lack of food Layla." Betty said as she peeled Layla off the car. "Come on, we got this far silly."

"Oh all right." Layla groaned. "I just don't want to clean up the house and then deal with Chance and oh," Layla sighed. "I don't want to now."

Betty gave Layla a stern look. Without saying anything, Layla got dressed and then into the driver's seat and started up the car. Betty hopped in and a way they went back up the road. When they arrived to the house, all seem to be quiet. The front door was wide open. No one was in the living room or the dining room. Where was everyone? Dawson's jeep was still parked outside.

"May be they all went hiking?" Betty said to Layla.

"I highly doubt that." Layla rolled her eyes. The two girls went upstairs. There they found Grunt, Allen, Dawson, Chance, and the two other guys. They were sleeping. "Sshhh..." Layla whispered. "Let's go raid the refrigerator."

Betty giggled as she followed Layla back down the stairs. When they entered the kitchen they had not a clue that Allen had followed them down. Or at least they didn't hear him sneak down the stairs behind them. Layla had opened the refrigerator door and took a peak. Hardly any food was left. Orange juice, a few old stinking left over's, an egg roll, a jar of olives, and a jar of mayonnaise. No bread in the bread drawer, no cereal in the cupboard, and no crackers. In the freezer there was nothing. Every frozen item was gone.

"Looks like we might need to go shopping." Allen said in the living room entry way. Both girls jumped.

"Crap Allen," Layla said catching her breath. "Stop sneaking up on us."

"You two are so loud." Allen laughed lightly.

"We were super quiet when we came in. I don't know how you heard us but you definitely were not asleep." Betty said to Allen.

"No." He admitted. "Dawson's feet smell like butt

and it is hard dream with that foul odor." He smiled. "I'm bored."

"Allen you are always bored." Layla smiled. "So it looks like we need some food in here." Layla grabbed the car keys. "Up for some shopping adventure?" She looked at Betty and Allen.

They both shrugged their shoulders and smiled. Layla led the way back to the front door and the three of them were off to the local grocery store.

They had fifteen minutes to shop before the grocery store closed. They didn't panic because Layla's step father owned the store and if they were still shopping the assistant manager would keep it open until Layla was finished foraging for food for the house. Now if it was Layla's step father's brother; that would have been in a panic. That man hated Layla, and Layla despised him. There was much conflicted between her and her uncle.

The three of them traveled down each isle of the small store picking out anything and everything that looked good. Chips, sauce packages, muffins, juice other than orange juice, milk, eggs, bacon, steaks, hamburger meat, lettuce, tomatoes, onions, sprouts, pop tarts, cereals of all sorts, ice cream, coffee, and crackers. There was so much stuffed into one small metal cart. Allen was pushing the cart and Layla was grabbing stuff. Betty was taking what Layla had and jamming it into the cart. Then the three would switch when they entered into another isle.

When they were through shopping it was ten minutes after closing time. The assistant manager checked out their purchases and had Layla sign a tab for her step father to pay later. Allen went outside and loaded up the car; both back seat and trunk were full of food. There was a tight squeeze for Allen to sit in the back. Betty and Layla stood still for the assistant manager to turn on the alarm in the store and then they made their exit. Allen had already broken into a bag of cookies to munch on as he smooched himself into the car. Betty flopped in a Depeche Mode tape to play and Layla drove off.

"That bill your dad will be paying for is pretty fat." Betty yelled over the music that was pounding through the speakers.

"Fuck him; I have a right to eat." Layla laughed. She wasn't being sarcastic either. She practically starves when her parents are at home. When they left like this weekend, Layla got to buy as much food as she pleased without her step father jumping down her throat about eating so much.

"Well," Allen said over the music, "now you won't starve for at least a month." He rummaged through one of the bags and opened up the Ho Ho box. He took out one of the individual wrapped pastries and stuffed it into his mouth. "Hey did you buy smokes?" He tried to say with a mouthful of chocolate and cream.

"Yes I bought two cartons." Layla said understanding him through the blare of the music.

"Good because you owe me like three packs." He smiled at Layla as she glanced into her rearview mirror. "Your parents should just give you this car. You drive it more than they do."

"Yeah right. They won't give me a car." Layla said as she made the turn down Pool Station Road. "They are too afraid I'd drive across the states." She laughed and Betty laughed with her.

"Would you really go across the states Layla?" Betty asked her.

"Hell yeah in heart beat just to get out of here." Layla said. She started to slow the car down to make the turn up the driveway towards the gate. "I don't want to be here anymore."

"What about you're Volkswagen?" Allen said as he unbuckled himself from his tight position in the backseat with groceries.

"You have a VW?" Betty asked.

"It doesn't run. It needs a lot of work." Layla sighed. She drove past the gate and towards the first flat. She would slightly swerve missing fresh cow poo. Dawson was visible at the first flat of the hill. He was sitting on the front porch smoking a cigarette.

"I'll fix it for you Layla." Allen chipped in. Betty turned down the song, Little Sixteen.

"Allen your parents would freak out if you stayed here just to fix a car." Layla smirked.

"Who cares about them. I know I could do it." Allen said to Layla. Betty was feeling a bit hot about this. She had feelings for Allen and really didn't want Layla spending alone time with him because she knew that Allen still liked Layla. Betty wouldn't have a chance.

Layla parked the car into the garage. Dawson came into the garage as Layla closed the automatic door behind them. She turned off the car and got out. Betty got out too and started to unload the car full of groceries. Where Allen went to no one seem to have noticed. It was as if he was at the house the entire time. Magical appearances? He was body doubling.

"Hey your mother called." Dawson said.

"Are they on their way home?" Layla asked

opening up the door.

"No. She was just checking in on you." Dawson told Layla.

"One of those things." Layla rolled her eyes and laughed. "She must have had a bad feeling and called. Oh well. Dawson," Layla said to him, "get the others to help out with the food."

Dawson ran around the corner and up the stairs to get the others. They slowly came down to help fill the house with food again. Layla, Allen, and Betty made one trip with groceries and then went into the living room to flop on the couches. They others started preparing dinner and putting things away. Still in the back of Betty's mind was the question of the blood. When everyone except the three of them were too busy to eavesdrop Betty asked Allen, "The night of the Love Fest," she whispered, "where did all that blood come from?" His eyes seem to narrow. Betty started to sweat.

"You don't know?" Allen said in a harsh whisper.

"No dumb ass this is why she is asking you." Layla grumbled at him.

"Do you know this answer Layla?" Allen was curious if Layla didn't realize.

"Truth." Layla said softly. "No. I have not a clue. So," she told him, "enlighten us."

"Whoa," He smiled in delight. "You girls have some deep issues." Allen said and with that he went silent and closed his eyes in a happy way.

"Allen?" Betty whined. "Tell us what you seen that night."

With his eyes closed and a smile bigger than the size of Texas he simply stated, "That was the best sex a man could ever have."

Layla was obviously upset. She stammered out of the room to help the others put away groceries. Betty just sat there staring at Allen in amusement. May be he won't tell Layla but he could possibly tell Betty. Maybe. Betty sat there in Allen's silent company as the others prepared dinner. The smell of steak was overwhelming but also inviting to Betty and Allen's senses. Chance was making macaroni salad with cubes of sliced cheese. Dawson was making mashed potatoes, and the other two guys were helping with what they could. Layla was attending to the steaks. Allen opened his eyes and jetted his sights on Betty who was watching him. He smiled a lazy smile at her and winked.

"Better than you." He said with an evil tone.

"What?" Betty said automatically before thinking of what he was talking about. "You are a pig." She finally said in a hot tone. "You'd rather have an orgy than one on one?"

"No I rather have variety than one on boring one." He then got up and went into the kitchen to help out.

Betty just sat there. She was dissed by Allen who had absolutely no heart for her at all. It was as if she had gone soft since that night of the Love Fest. What happened to her? She felt as if she was weak. Not weak in a physical sense but weak in a spiritual sense. Her powers of craft couldn't ever compare to Layla's. Why? What made her so beautiful and so powerful? Jealousy rose up in Betty like lava does in a volcano. She would make Allen hers if it was the last thing she would do. Allen will love her. Betty vowed this in her thoughts. She sat there watching Allen flirt with Layla and there Layla was being cruel to him as usual. Layla didn't deserve him. Why is he so devoted to her? Why? This question screamed in Betty's mind as she watched him.

Allen had set up the table, Chance and Dawson arranged the food in the center. Dinner was done. Betty just sat there listening to all of them. "Betty come on aren't you hungry?" Chance yelled out.

"Yeah I'll be right there." Betty managed to say back. She got up from the couch and headed into the dining room. She took a seat next to Grunt who actually ate dainty for what he looked like. Small girlish bites for such a tough talker. Then again he wasn't talking much lately.

She filled her plate with food. She watched more than she ate. Betty watched Allen eat and glance every now and again at Layla. Layla was involved with what was on her plate rather than paying any attention to those around her. Chance was playing footsies with one of the strange guys and talking to the other guy about cars. Dawson was also observing the room full of eaters. Betty smiled at Dawson but he didn't even flinch. His stare went from Betty to Chance and the rest of them. Betty poked at her potatoes remembering Ava and what they had the other night. Then she poked at the meat on her plate. The steak was juicy. The more fork holes she put into it the more it ran a pretty hue of red. Little oil droplets spewed out with the juice making a pattern on the white plate. It started to mix with the macaroni salad and became pink in color.

Betty did finally eat but only after Allen, Layla, Grunt, Chance and those two guys left the table to put their dishes in the dishwasher. Dawson was left staring at Betty. They both were eating slowly, except Dawson was still staring.

"What Dawson?" Betty finally asked him.

"You are into witchcraft aren't you?" Dawson asked as he put another bite of mashed potatoes into his mouth.

"So." Betty shrugged.

"Ha." He said, "you dark little devil you." He then smiled.

"You are being strange Dawson." Betty told him as she tried now to hurry up.

"Me strange? No no," he said as he kept staring and eating at the same time in a creepy manner. "you and your friends are weird. That thing we did last night was freakish. I don't know? You all give me bad vibes." With that he took his stare away from her and paid more attention to his food.

"Thanks Dawson." Betty said shaking her head at him. At least he was being truthful. Betty finished her food and went into the kitchen. Chance was making out with one of those guys. The other guy, Layla and Allen were outside cracking up. Betty took her plate to the sink. "Hey Chance, get a room." Betty said.

"Yeah I've heard that one before." and Chance went back to kissing the dude.

Betty managed to make her way outside to see why the others were laughing. Not much to it, they were laughing at Chance. They were watching her from the window.

Betty took a seat at the red picnic table out on the patio. She watched Layla and her friends laugh and stare and talk about Chance. There on the picnic table was a pack of smokes. She lit one up and inhaled deeply. Dawson finally managed to join the crowd outside. He sat at the other end of the table and lit up a cigarette too. Inside the kitchen, through the window, Dawson and Betty watched not only Chance and that guy make out but there stood Grunt who was trying not to disturb them as he made coffee. Dawson and Betty started to laugh at Grunt; he had funny expressions on his face every time Chance kicked up her leg from sitting on the countertop. Or when the guy would bump into Grunt with his elbow or hand. It was becoming a comedy.

REVENGE

The phone rang unexpectedly. Layla and Allen raced inside to answer it. Layla who tripped Allen coming into the sliding door had reached the phone first as Allen just laid there laughing hysterically on the linoleum floor.

Chapter Seven

"Hello" Layla greeted the caller. "I'm not sure, I'll need to ask. Hold on." She turned towards everyone and asked, "Who is up for a night excursion?"

Dawson looked at Betty. Betty shrugged her shoulders. Allen who was still on the floor had propped himself up and said "I'm in for an outing."

Chance; who was still stuck to the lips of a guy, raised her hand. She was in. But the guy tried to keep her hand from flying up. He was out. Grunt was eagerly shaking his head in a yes. He was in. The other guy said, "Sure there isn't anything else to do and I don't want to watch another one of your bizarre movies. No offense Layla, but they are cheesy." He was in.

Layla returned to the conversation that was on the phone. "They all said yes.... Okay, we'll be there." and she hung up the phone.

"Who was that?" Grunt asked Layla.

"J Dog." Layla smiled. "May be this time he'll give us that damn map." She started to laugh.

Grunt grabbed a traveling cup for his coffee. Allen, Betty, and Dawson started gathering into the garage. Chance peeled herself away from the guy she was kissing and he followed. The other guy waited for Layla and came into the garage with her. They all piled into the Thunderbird. Four in the back, three in the front, and Allen stuffed into the trunk of the car. Why? The reason was totally unknown but it was sure funny. Betty stuck in the tape of Soup Dragons and a way they went down the drive way out towards the road. Layla took some back roads and headed out towards the graveyard. It was the larger graveyard which was located above the high school. Layla parked the car at a friend's house and everyone piled out of it. Allen was kicking the trunk to get their attention. No one forgot him but maybe he thought that.

The group filed into a line to squeeze their way through the fence that was partially open. Into the dark night they made their way up to a much larger crowd of people who were drinking. J Dog and the rest of their misfit friends were laughing and making a small fire pit. A preppy crowd stood around drinking and passing a pipe packed with weed. Layla somehow got a group to gather around a grave. Ava was there and she had joined the group. Someone brought black pillar candles and had set them into a circle on top of the black shiny marble of the grave. What was Ava doing at a function like this? Ava even joined into the ritual. A Christian at a séance?

Betty decided to join this group of intrigue. Layla had everyone sit down around the candles and hold hands. The others that were there partying and starting a bon fire got silent. They were all interested in what this small group was doing.

Layla looked upon the circle of people. "Now is the time to focus on what is not now." With that she bowed her head. Betty and the others bowed their heads also. Even Ava bowed her head. Layla said a few Coven words which no one understood except for those who knew of the Coven. The candles that burned slow and steady began to flicker. Then they started to burn a shade of blue. In the shiny black marble of the grave a shape took form in the reflection. Those who were standing about watching were amazed at this. It was human. A lady.

"Holy shit." one guy said as he stood there watching the shape take form in the smooth marble. The marble rippled like water in its circular form. The candles stood at its edges as if it held the water in its place. The circle of people began to softly sway back and forth and there was a hum of excitement. The lady whose reflection was in the marble began to come out of the rippling marble. She was still a reflection on rock as she surfaced. As soon as her hand came out of the rock she took on a ghostly form and stepped out of her reflective prison. The marble stopped rippling as she took her last step out. The marble became solid again. She was transparent, elusive, and beautiful. Her aura was powerful and an illuminant radiated around her. Again someone from the standing crowd said something. The lady looked up at them with a stern face.

"Who are you?" Ava said in wonderment.

The lady was as if she was the very breath of air flown into each person in the circle until she found a body empty of the now. She was a soul. Through the person she spoke, "I am that of what not is today."

Another person in the circle asked, "Are you from this graveyard?"

The lady spoke again, "No. But I assure you I am dead."

Layla then asked, "Who are you here for?"

The lady then answered, "For Betty and for you."

Betty then asked, "Why us?"

"Layla run away. Do not accepted to be the chosen one. You are much too powerful than Him." The lady said this as the body of the person started to fight the soul. "Betty fly to the gates of hell. There we shall meet again with Ava." and the person whom the spirit entered bit the other person next to her in order to break the hands that were being held. The person started to scream in pain as the soul was being ripped out of her and back into the black shiny marble grave. Those who were not part of the séance were bedazzled and they all started to talk about it.

Those who were in the small circle got up and laughed at the one who was bitten. The girls hand was okay but the bite mark was red and swollen. Layla just sat there with her knees up to her chin rocking back and forth. Betty sat by Layla. She didn't say anything, she just watched Layla rock back and forth. She wondered what it all meant when the spirit told Layla to run away.

"I should go home now Layla." Betty finally said.

"Why so you can fly to the gates of hell tonight?" Layla spouted off. She turned to Betty and gave her a vicious look. "She didn't tell you to run away."

"What?" Betty felt a deep hollowness burned into her heart. "Who cares what this 'thing' you summoned up said. I don't understand you at times. One minute you are the coolest chic alive and I'm jealous of you and then the next minute you are this other person who I hate." Betty scooted over some to fill her vision with

Layla's rocking profile. "Fly to the gates of hell. I don't even know what that means."

"Do you recall your dreams Betty?" Layla asked. She was still hot under her breath about the situation.

"No. Why?" Betty said hotly, knowing deep down this was what kept her weak in power.

"Try to. At least tonight, try to remember." Layla stopped rocking and she stretched out her long willowy legs against the black marble of the grave. "I can't believe you don't remember what you are going through." Layla put her hands in back of her to balance her upper body in a lounge position.

"And just what am I going through Layla?" Betty asked her in sarcasm. "I really don't think you know."

"Betty." Layla said as her eyes turned that wild lime green. "I know more than you are thinking. I know your subconscious as well as your conscience and sometimes your deepest thoughts are louder than you can imagine so stop screaming at me okay."

Betty just stared at her friend. If fire could be spit out of her eyes, it would have landed on Layla and caught her aflame. She was ferrous. Layla smiled at Betty. Betty got up, dusted herself off and left. Most of the crowd was going their separate ways by this time. Layla just sat there watching Betty walk away. Betty was so angry. She met up with a group of misfit friends that were going somewhere else to drink and party. Her bay area boyfriend was with them.

They all headed down the road from the graveyard and across the street to the elementary school. It was like the night was a living essence. Betty could feel her nerves ache for adrenaline. A friend handed her a bottle of Southern Comfort and she pounded it down like it was water. They all walked up towards the lunch area and her bay area boyfriend took out his skateboard that was attached to his backpack. A few other skaters took out their boards and started to skate.

The stoner girls along with Betty drank and watched as the boys did tricks over walking ramps, steps, and hand rails. Betty felt her world spinning. She chased after her boyfriend and took his board.

"Ha!" She giggled at him as she tore him off the board. "My turn you turd!"

She joined the guys skating down the steep slope and jumping the low chain fence. Drunk and stupor a lot of them crashed and burned. Laughter rose in the still night air. Betty made it over the chain and went around the corner. Still spinning with drunken delight she grabbed a low hanging net that was provided for shade. She pulled herself up on the jungle like canopy.

"Heya!" She laughed. The skateboard went skirting off down the hill. "I'm now on the top of all you fools." She said to some of the skater boys who flew under her.

The guy thought what she did was cool so they joined her and the net came tumbling down. A few guys and Betty landed on the pavement laughing at the incident of making havoc of school property. Her vision was becoming blurred. Body started to slow and become immobile from the alcohol. When she went to get up she fell back down. Somehow Allen was there. He helped her get back up on her feet.

"Allen?" Betty slurred his name.

"Layla kicked us out." He said as he carried Betty to a nearby bench. "Says her parents were on their way home."

"Do you believe that?" Betty asked him as she took a seat with his guidance.

"No." He smiled. "I think something spooked her." Allen sat next to Betty. "Hey, I'm sorry for pissing you off tonight."

Betty's mood was fuzzy. She didn't know what to think of this. "I shouldn't have been so into you. I have a boyfriend but I can't tell him everything."

"Your boyfriend is cheating on you." Allen said as he stretched out his long legs and leaned up against the bench back. "Well, he will end up cheating on you. He will know your secrets soon."

"Allen." Betty said trying to swallow the thickness that built up in her throat. "I think I'm going to be sick." She leaned over just in case.

"No you aren't going to get sick." Allen said putting his hand on her head. "Thalca Ti Dephacea." He casted a spell.

Betty was feeling the lump in her throat slowly disappear. Her head started to clear up. She shook off the fuzziness. Betty then came back up from leaning over and looked at Allen. "Thanks." She said with a sheepish smile.

"Let's talk." He said as he recoiled himself from stretched out to getting up. "We should go to the field and walk the track."

"We'll avoid the puke fest over there where your boyfriend is." Allen started to laugh.

"Did you cast a spell on them?" Betty said with curiosity. "Because they were doing just fine when we were skating."

"No I didn't do it." Allen said leading Betty towards the track. "Grunt did."

"You guys can be so heartless." Betty smirked.

"Sometimes you have to be heartless. It is what makes you stronger." He told her.

When they arrived onto the track that circled the field, they both slowed their pace in a rhythmic walk. Slow and settle. The night air felt good on Betty's bare legs. The coolness of the grass whipped up through the slight breeze and the scents of pond water rose from it.

Allen started up the conversation. His eyes were focused ahead like looking into the future for words. "I love Layla and I want to show her what she will be missing if I am taken. I want her to miss me so much that she becomes lonely."

Betty felt his hurt. His heart was in some major pain. Layla and her games were going to back fire on her. "So," she said, "why are you telling me this?" Betty already had the feeling of what he was about to ask.

"I want to go out with you. Spend the rest of this summer with you." He said.

She knew it. There was going to be a war between Layla and Allen. Anyone involved would get hurt or worse. She didn't care. After what Layla pulled tonight, she was in for it. "Okay." she said. "I'll be your girlfriend. But I have to break up with my boyfriend I already have first."

They both laughed. Allen then said, "He already cheated on you. Just now. He's having some black mocha right now."

"Allen?" Betty was laughing but it wasn't really funny. That black mocha was her African American friend. "Where is he?" She asked.

"Over in the hallway by the bathrooms." Allen said.

Betty stopped. She looked over towards the locked bathrooms. The hallway light was put out. Mysteriously put out. She then glanced at Allen with an evil grin. "Let's catch them." Betty said.

"Ha!" He laughed. "Let's." and the two of them ran up to the dark hallway.

There the two were. Betty's girly friend and her boyfriend. Betty and Allen were quiet and they watched. They started to giggle. The girl turned around. She was half naked against the wall. The boyfriend wasn't even paying attention.

"Shit Betty!" The girl shouted as she pushed the boyfriend away from her body. "I'm so sorry. I felt bad for him after he puked and it just happened. I didn't want to but..." She was trying to explain.

Allen broke in and said, "Who cares. Betty is mine now."

The boyfriend was pulling up his pants and looked at Allen. "The fuck she is bitch." He was stumbling and Allen started to laugh.

"Dude," Allen said, "You are so drunk you can't do anything about it." Then he ended the sentence, "BITCH"

The cheating boyfriend got into Allen's face. "You touch her and you die."

"Already did. Last night and other nights before that so what's it to you?" Allen was starting up a fight. He was also in the guys face staring him down ready to brawl.

"Allen please don't." Betty whispered. "He has a black belt Allen. Don't do it."

"Yeah." Allen said with an evil laugh. "I have this." and with his hands came a small electric spark.

"You're dead." The boyfriend said and he pushed Allen away, cocked his fist and was about to fling it at Allen's face.

Allen sparked up again. It was the coolest thing in the dark hallway. When the fist came flying, the electric sparks came shooting out and hit the boyfriend in the gut. The cheating boyfriend went down. Allen did it again and again. He was laughing insanely while torturing the boyfriend. Again and again.

"I'm Fry Guy. Feel my fire you fuck!" Allen laughed in a mad rage.

The girly friend of Betty's shouted, "Stop it Allen you'll kill him!"

Allen kept doing it despite what she shouted. The misfit friends came up to watch. The electric sparks ended and Allen was now kicking the cheating boyfriend hard. Each kick threw the guy further out into eyes view into the lunch area. Finally Grunt and Betty pulled Allen away from the limp and suffering body.

"Geez Allen you almost killed him." one friend out of the crowd said.

"He won't die. He'll suffer in life for a long ass time before he dies." Allen said.

"Come on Allen." Betty was giggling in amusement. "We should leave before the cops come."

Grunt, Allen, and Betty took off hitch hiking to Allen's house. Indeed the cops did show up at the elementary school but the three of them were not there. All their misfit friends got into trouble that night. For a while during the summer days it was just Allen, Grunt, and Betty. They did a lot of hanging out in the small town of Mokel. A town which highway 49 ran through, and if you blinked you'd have missed driving by it.

It must have been morning in the hospital. Betty had drifted off to sleep. She was restless because of the pain. None of the medications the nurses gave her was working. Every now and again Ava would watch her friend twitch and hear her moan. Ava, who didn't want to hear any of this, stayed anyway. Betty wasn't going to talk about it unless Ava was in the room with her. So, instead of feeling the emotions and hearing about the sickness, Ava blocked it out and thought of other things. Was this crazy talk real? Ava doubted it. Or did she doubt?

"Did you make a few phone calls?" Trent asked his wife.

"Yeah." She smiled lightly. "I got a hold of Layla. Had to track her down on the Internet. Allen was the same way. Grunt can't be found."

"Did you call Betty's father?" Trent asked. "He'll want to know that she doesn't have long to live now."

"Trent," Ava said in sorrow, "I..." She paused. "I can't call that man." Ava started to cry. "You call him. I'm sorry." Ava turned towards the window.

"I'll call him." Trent said gently. "We'll need to know how Betty wants her funeral. I have a feeling she might not make it out of here."

"I know." Ava sighed.

"When is Layla coming?" Trent asked Ava who was still staring out the window.

"Soon." Ava said.

"Where did you find her?" Trent was curious.

"You'll never believe me if I told you. I had to pay a hundred and sixty dollars just to locate her." She smiled with the thought of what Layla was doing today.

"So? Where did you find her Honey? I really would like to know too." Trent giggled.

"She is a part of the Church." Ava said finally facing her husband.

"What? Layla the 'High Priestess' a part of a Church?" Trent was amazed.

"Not just any type of Church." Ava said with a corky smile. "She is a Nun for a Catholic Church. Well, going to be a Nun anyway. She is a Sister now." Ava started to giggle.

"I'm a Pastor and she is a Sister. Isn't that funny how life turns around for the greater good?" He smiled enjoying the grace of God. "She was so wild back then. I'm glad that she is doing well."

"It is strange. I do remember her summoning up that glow from the grave. Now she is a Sister. Boy, did we do some growing up." Ava said.

Trent and Ava were sitting at a small table in Betty's hospital room. They were drinking coffee and talking. They were enjoying the late morning. Betty kept stirring around in her sleep. The nurse would come in and check up on things and then leave. The smell of food came from the long hallway when the door would open. Once in a while they would hear someone in pain or the intercom paging a doctor. Finally Layla came into the room. Trent was so shocked to see Layla dressed in a Nun's outfit.

"Ava?" Layla said in a hesitant voice.

"Layla? Wow look at you." Ava said almost crying. "You look so different without make up."

Both ladies were laughing at that. Ava got up and approached Layla. Layla gave Ava a hug and patted her back as if she was a child.

"Ava you are so funny." Layla said. "And I believe this is Trent from high school?" Layla asked.

"Hi Layla. I know we didn't really see much of each other in high school." Trent said as he gave her a hug also.

"A Pastor. Very good Ava. Nice choice!" Layla said

with a big smile. "I'm so sorry to hear about Betty. Poor thing. She just couldn't get away from all that. Huh." Layla then turned to Betty who was still asleep. Layla had sadness in her eyes. "Oh the precious thing. What exactly happened? May be we should go somewhere else. I don't want to disturb her rest." Layla said putting her hand on Betty's head.

"We could go outside and talk. That might be good." Trent said. "She has been stirring around this morning. She fell asleep about two hours ago. Up all night talking." Trent opened the door for the two ladies. Ava led the way out to the benches not too far from the hospital entry way.

"Up talking all night?" Layla was confused. "She shouldn't talk. She needs her strength to heal."

"She is healing." Trent said softly. "She's confessing her sins. She stayed up telling Ava and I of her troubles." His face was solemn. Did Layla turn to God in order to save her soul too? Did she still remember what happened back then?

"Confessing." Layla said. Her facial expression was straight. "I too confessed my sins to God."

Ava broke into this conversation. "She told us about the Coven. Coven 82. Do you remember this?"

The three of them approached the benches and

sat down in a huddled little group. Layla had her hands tucked inside her robe sleeves. She was looking at the faces of Ava and Trent. She smiled a small insecure smile.

"Yes." She whispered. "I remember."

"Did you do those blood thirsty things Layla?" Trent just had to ask.

"There is no need for me to go back to the past. I am forgiven of all those things. What Betty remembers is of her own sins. She should lay them to rest at God's feet." Layla said still smiling.

"So there was blood drinking and orgies?" Ava said in disguised.

"There were many things. As I recall you participated in a few of them Ava. What do you remember?" Layla said looking at her through cold steel blue eyes.

"All I remember was the ghost. It was strange. That is all I remember." Ava looked a bit nervous. There was something more than just ghost tales with Ava.

Trent looked at his wife with concern. Did he miss something?

"Well." Trent said with a deep sigh. "I thought maybe you'd tell us more about Coven 82. Betty is dying. She has internal bleeding. It's slow but it is shutting off her kidney functions and she has liver damage from all this. Whatever drugs and alcohol she consumed has done her in."

"What exactly happened to her?" Layla asked again.

"Suicide after drinking and doing some drugs." Ava told her. "She lit herself on fire, jumped off a building and had a rope around her neck. It was an incredible suicide attempt. Now she is slowly going nuts before she passes away."

"Strange suicide." Layla's smile disappeared. She looked around her. Then she got close to Trent and Ava. She whispered, "Did Betty mention any names? Any foreign names?"

"Hasbrath." Ava blurted out.

"SSHHH!" Layla waved her hand and gave Ava a stern look.

"What?" Ava said in that teenage snotty tone.

"Saying these names is like awaking the Demons." Layla whispered. "That name especially." Layla then went back to a relaxed position on the bench. With a normal tone in her voice she asked them, "Have you ever heard of The Venice Code? Oh you could call it the Venus Code. Whichever one suits you."

"You mean about Mary and all that nonsense." Trent laughed. "Sure, there are several books about it. Fictional books that people are following today. The Rose Path, and saying she is Queen."

"Yes. Nonsense. Unless you are summoning up the Queen of Hell." Layla smiled that insecure smile. She was nervous being at the hospital. "See, we were in search for this Queen."

"So what happened?" Ava asked in excitement.

"Surely Betty will tell you." Layla said. "I should go for now. I have many things to do and so little time."

Chapter Eight

Ava and Trent watched as Layla walked away. They were shocked that she became such a religious lady. She turned her faith around after all that Coven garbage. Was it seriously real? They were bewildered. They went back to Betty's room. Betty was wide awake and fighting off nurses, screaming and kicking.

"Why the hell did you leave me alone?" She yelled at Ava.

"It was only for a moment Betty. Please settle down." Ava went to Betty's bedside and sat down in the chair. "No one is going to hurt you in here." Ava reassured her.

"The Elders," Betty said in a frantic voice, "they are judges, lawyers, and doctors. You don't know until they face you. They weren't all teenagers you know."

"Alright Betty." Ava said as she reached towards Betty's hand to hold it.

"Please don't leave me alone again. Please I beg you." Betty started to cry.

"Layla was here." Ava told her. "She thought you might need rest." Ava was caressing Betty's hand.

"Layla." Betty repeated the name. "Is she?" Betty started to panic and it made the heart monitor wild.

"No no." Ava said softly. "She turned her life around. She is a Nun now in the Catholic Church. There is nothing to be afraid of."

"I had hurt her real bad you know." Betty said in a whisper.

Trent, who was standing behind Ava, was listening. He had the urge to ask Betty. "How did you hurt Layla? She didn't mention any of this that you've been talking about. Only of Hasbrath and the Venice or Venus Code."

"The Venus Code. Mary." Betty repeated. Her heart rate went down. She started to drift off into another memory. "You remember the Ouija ball? The name Mary which ties into Hasbrath. The ghost in the graveyard. The Harvest." Betty turned to Trent.

Trent with full eye contact on Betty walked to the other side of Betty's death bed. He took a seat. Betty followed every move of Trent. Only her eyes followed him and then her head pointed to his direction. It was evil the way she did that. Spooky.

"I remember." Ava said so that Betty didn't look at her husband in that manner. "You didn't tell us about The Harvest though."

Betty was in the Mokel Park. A small park with large shade trees, an awning that led up to the Main Street, a picnic table, and the place was tucked around the corner. She was waiting for J Dog and Allen. She had been staying with a girl named Alice. A new girl with a whole new crowd of friends. It was early in the summer morning. It felt good to wear shorts and have her hair up off her back. She was restful and at peace since her and Allen were seeing each other.

Allen could be heard from his backyard screaming at J Dog. "Come on you dick!"...."No you fried monkey, let's just get the hell out of here!" Then moments later Allen showed up without the notorious J Dog.

"Where is the pussy?" Betty laughed. "He is so chicken." She got up from off the lawn and came up to Allen. They greeted with a short but sultry kiss and an embrace.

"He doesn't want to go swimming. I even told him that there would be chic's in bikinis and he still won't come." Allen shook his head. "He better not be digging around and tearing up books again or my dad will shit his pants." He took Betty by the hand and they both sat on top of the picnic table.

"Smoke?" Betty said with a smile.

"Sure. Gotta die of something right." Allen said as he took the cigarette from out of Betty's pack of Marlboro's.

"We'll never die my love." She said in a cute voice. "We'll live forever young." She lit up her smoke by the courtesy of Allen's lighter.

Then he lit up his own. "You'll die. According to the numbers you will die young. No children, unwed, and frightened." He turned to her and kissed her.

She broke away from the kiss. "What? How do you know all this?" She asked taking a drag of her cigarette.

"It is in the numbers." He said as he twitched. "See, I take your birth date and add them to the letters of your birth right name,"

Before he said anymore Betty started to laugh out loud. "Allen," she said, "I don't care. Just as long as I have fun now. Like I said, forever young." and she kissed him back viciously.

J Dog finally did arrive up to the park. The three of them sat there waiting for their ride to the river to go swimming. The entire day was nothing but making out with Allen and swimming. Smoking weed with a few other new friends and jumping off the rocks. Grunt showed up an hour before they all left the place. Now there were four of them. They ended up at Allen's house. Night was sneaking up on them quicker than expected. J Dog returned to his trailer that was in the back of Allen's house.

Grunt, Allen, and Betty prepared for an interesting night where Jesus Maria Road was.

The Harvest

The entire 85 Covens were there this night. August 23, 1993. An interesting fact, August is the eighth month of the year. Add two and three which equals to the fascinating number thirteen. Now Menod Natsatis has four types of women in mind. Add one, nine, nine, and the number three together. The conclusion is obvious. The number four for four females to fill the place of a Queen. One will rule the kingdom of hell.

All the witches were cloaked. There were others, including some of Betty's new found friends. They were dressed normally and they were there to party and watch. Tonight was the night. Betty was excited. Their Coven, Coven 82, stood in a small group by the giant bon fire. They were doing their normal chanting to summon up "guardians" or the children of Hasbrath. These "guardians", soul like creatures, would enter into whoever wanted it from the non coven crowd. They didn't know it, but they were their sacrifice.

Layla, Allen, and Grunt chose a few of the non coven people to join their Coven. The Elders laid hands on them chanting an ancient chant. The black cloaked Coven witches gathered around and laid hands on the Elders. The red cloaked witches enclosed around them and raised their arms to the universe. They drew out their daggers from their cloaks. All thirteen of them and pierced the skin of those who were not of the coven. They gathered this into a silver decorated cup. The Highest Elder then went to the only white cloaked witch in the crowd and offered it to this witch.

All the females who were chosen went up to the huge fire. They joined hands and kneeled in a neat tight circle. Betty was shuffled in this crowd and lost Layla somewhere. She was holding hands with strangers from another Coven Region. Betty kneeled with them. The white cloaked one chanted and as if on automatic, all the girls whipped back their cloaks. Heads down, bodies shown. In the background you could hear faint whispers of non coven people. There must have been about a hundred of them.

Then out came a fawn. Every Elder got together and ran their hands over the scared animal. It was led by a rope and handed to the white cloaked one. Some sort of prayer was said and every Coven thanked "Their Lord". All the red cloaked ones that were not chosen took their daggers and stuck the poor innocent animal. Blood spilled and was caught by some sort of other rather large animal skin. All those who were wearing black cloaks and were not chosen took a piece of this skin and rubbed it on those who were chosen and connected by hand holding around a huge fire.

The chant was on. Loud in the foothills. The fire burned bright out in the pitch blackness. Smoke, black and thick from the fire rose up into the velvet dark blue sky fading out the stars. Betty felt the moist skin being swept across her naked body. All the skins were thrown in the fire. Betty and the other chosen girls started to chant. They were weaving back and forth on their knees to the beautiful chanting as if hypnotized. Like a snake being summoned out of its basket by a flute. They were once again covered in blood.

The white cloaked witch walked slowly behind each kneeling chosen female. Every now and again Betty could see that a hand would touch one of their bowed heads. With that, the female would faint. She anticipated her turn. What if she wasn't chosen? Only one female per Coven? What if Layla is chosen? The ones that didn't get touched by this white cloaked figure was lifted up from out of the circle and led by the Elders into the darkness.

Which one was Layla? There were two other red cloaked females left and a bunch who wore black. The white cloaked figure touched a red cloaked girl and she went down. There were only four red cloaked ones who were touched. The other red cloaked female left the group. The white cloaked figure passed up Betty but touched the girl next to her. The girls hand burned instantly and Betty had to release the hand. Then she felt herself being lifted up to stand by blue cloaked figures and she was led away from the hot intense bonfire.

They led her to a tree by a few other now not so chosen females. They tied her up. Arms stretched upwards, cloak thrown back for all to see her nakedness. The other tied up girls were moaning in some sort of pain. Sorrow? Betty didn't want to fear this or even fight it. They tied her feet and left her to pick up the other now not so chosen girls. Suddenly Betty felt it. Sleep. It came on fast.

"Remember your dreams Betty." A familiar voice whispered to her. It was Allen who snuck up out of the darkness and by her side. She fell into the blackness of empty dreams. "Remember" she heard him but it was distant now.

Flying High

She was flying over a forest. Soaring, catching wind. She reared up her head to feel the sunlight but all she could feel was coldness. She came close to the ground and stood small in such a dark and cold forest. She felt sadness, hurt, and loneliness. Why? She tried to walk but all she could do was hop. What was this? She glanced down at herself. She was a bird. A small bird. A sparrow of sorts.

She looked around to see why she could feel these emotions. There in a distance, a meadow. She flew to a nearby tree that overlooked the meadow. She saw them, the ones who had fainted by the fire. They bowed their heads and kneeled. They were facing a small opening. A dark hollow with mist rising from it. A man came out. Naked and perfect. Betty felt as if she shouldn't look at him. Something about him was not right. So she directed her bird eyes to the females who were kneeling. All of them were naked as well.

They were chanting in praise. He walked among them. Then there in the trees hung those who were not chosen by that white cloaked figure. They hung by their necks like dolls. Lifeless. Betty twitched on the tree limb she was perched on. Out of fear she flew away. It could have been her! Her hanging lifeless from a tree. She flew over to the huge rot iron gate. Something about this gate she was to meet someone. Who? Who was she to meet by the gate? Was she able to go out into the rolling green lawn on the other side of this gate? She hopped towards the gate. Nervously, she gave it a thought. Would someone catch her doing this?

As always, she was sucked back to the waking hours. Betty opened her eyes. Allen's house. She was in Allen's bed. She was naked. She propped herself up and looked under the covers.

"You've seen it before Betty." Allen said with a smile. His eyes were closed and he was still a bit groggy.

"Why am I not covered in blood?" She asked as she looked at her body.

"We took a shower together last night." His arm came around and he wrapped himself onto her middle. He rested his head on her belly. He moaned a good moan.

"I don't remember that Allen." She told him.

"Might have been the concoction the Elders gave you to drink when you fell asleep all tied up. I'm surprised you made it back actually." He opened his big blue eyes and smiled up at her. She ran her fingers through his soft blond hair.

"What do you mean by that?" She asked him in concern.

"Well unfortunately those who were not chosen from last night will never come back mentally right in the head. They will forever suffer some delusion." He then buried his head between her white pale thighs. Allen wrapped his arms around her legs and poked his head up out of the covers from the bed. "You on the other hand are still here mentally. Did you remember this time?"

"I was a bird." She started to describe to him. "I saw the ones whom weren't chosen dangling from their necks in the trees." Then she arched herself up against his headboard. He was teasing her pleasure zone. "Allen!" She softly moaned, "We're gonna walk up your sister and brother you dork. Knock it off." Then Betty closed her legs on him.

"Ah no play?" He was laughing at her. "I need you Layla." He said in such a mistake.

Betty turned white as a ghost. "Layla?" With that she got out of his bed and put on her clothes. "We've been together for a month and you've never said her name until now. How dare you think of her when you are with me!" Her voice raised high.

"What are you talking about Betty?" He tried to hide it but it didn't work.

"You are such a game player." Betty said and her eyes flashed that wild silver. "One minute you are so in love with me and then the next minute you still think of her. Why her? What does she have that I don't have huh?" Betty slipped on her shoes and stood over him like a dark haired angel with a scowl on her face. "Is it the sex? Is it just because you like being used by her? She hates you Allen. She just uses you because you are easy." She crossed her arms. "I love you damn it and if you can't love me then this whole relationship means nothing." and with that she left his room.

She slammed his bedroom door. His brother and sister were sitting in the living room and they watched her go to the front door. She slammed that one too. She went up the street, towards the highway and started to hitch hike back to St. Andrews. Betty was going to Layla's house to face her. How dare Allen still be stuck on Layla after all that the two of them have been through during the summer. Layla deserves shit. She didn't care about anyone but herself and what made her so God damned special anyway?

Betty had enough of this nonsense. She was in hopes that Layla was one of those girls hanging like lifeless dolls from the forest trees. So what if she was a bird. Being a helpless scared bird saved her from going insane in the head. May be Layla lost it and went nuts! Yeah, that would just make Betty's day. Then Allen can take care of his precious Layla for the rest of his stupid dumb life. Oh the anger built up inside of Betty was just going to burst like black rain from a dark evil cloud that had been floating by heavily far too long now.

Dawson drove by. Betty put her head down along with her hitch hiking thumb. Oh not Dawson. He stopped down the highway. Then reversed the jeep. Betty just stood there as he swerved around her. This was going to be a bad day.

"Hey Betty, long time no see." He yelled out the window. He grabbed the door handle and tried to open the door while sitting in the driver's seat.

"Dawson." Betty said with a fake smile. "What are you doing today?" She came up to the jeep passenger door and opened it for him so that he'd stop struggling.

"Not much. Going into St. Andrews Town to drop

off some paperwork for my mom at the courthouse and then hanging out with Chance." He smiled. "Going that way?"

"Yes." She said trying not to look at him directly.

"Well dork hop on in. I'll give yeah a ride." He was chirpy.

"Thanks Dawson." and with that Betty hopped into his jeep. Incredible how things over the summer have changed. Dawson was hanging out with Chance? Too astonishing. Betty sat uncomfortable in the passenger seat. The hum of the vehicle on the road and silence.

"So grab a tape to listen to Betty." Dawson finally said to her.

"Where are they?" She was looking around. He pointed to a general direction to locate his collection of music and she laughed. "Dah, I'm an idiot. You own a lot of R&B here. Wow, haven't heard this song in a while." Betty popped in DRS.

"So, what brings you to these parts of the wood Betty?" Dawson asked her as he drove like a maniac down highway 26 towards St. Andrew.

"I've been stuck in Mokel for a while and I have some unresolved issues to clear up with Layla." She said with an evil grin.

"Ah," Dawson sighed, "yeah I think we all have unresolved issues with that snotty little brat." Then he laughed.

"Really? So, like I'm not the only one who hates her?" Betty smirked.

"Nope." Dawson said. "Ever since that stupid shit in the graveyard. Man, she can really hurt her friends." He shook his head.

"What did she do to you?" Betty asked out of curiosity.

"Well let's see." He said steering the wheel with one hand and trying to light a cigarette with the other. He inhaled, and then exhaled the gray smoke like a chimney. "She totally kicked us out of her house that night. Said her parents were coming home. But that wasn't the real issue. The real issue was that she and Allen were making out and he got a little rough with her." He took another drag. "She deserved it though because when we came back from the graveyard she started in on him. She pounced him before he had the chance to get out of the car. They were practically doing it in that trunk. When he didn't want to make out with her anymore, she started to pout and get nasty with us at the house. Then Allen decided to take her parents car for a joyride but it ended up in a fight."

"So that is what happened." Betty laughed. "Well," She started to tell Dawson, "Allen and I ended up together over at the elementary school that night. He told me that he loved her but it wasn't worth sticking around for. He even said that if he were to date other women then maybe she would see what she was missing."

"Oh," Dawson said, "you were his pawn then?" He made the turn on Gold Strike Road.

"Pawn?" Betty was confused. "Is that what I am to him?" Now she was really ruffled. If she could be a cat right now, her fur would've been fluffed.

"See Betty," Dawson said, "Think of it this way. Layla is a player of this huge game. She is into something really large. Larger than us okay. So is Allen. It is like a chess game. They gather these pieces or people and then play them on this board. But what they don't understand and some day they will, is that board will turn around on them." Dawson started taking the back roads of St. Andrew to the courthouse. "Life will get ugly for them and they don't grow up soon they'll be stuck in this game forever."

There was some truth in what Dawson was saying. Allen and Layla were stuck in a game that the Elders created. But who was bigger than the Elders?

Who was the white cloaked figure at The Harvest? Betty was going to get to the bottom of it and she had to do it quickly before she was played for a fool again.

"Thanks Dawson for the good advice." She sincerely smiled this time.

He parked his jeep in the court parking lot. "No problem Betty." He smiled back. "Well see yeah around."

"Sure." Betty said as she hopped out of the jeep. She went her way and Dawson went his. She headed towards Layla's but she wasn't going to face her. Not yet. The timing wouldn't be right. She was going to spy on the bitch. Where was Layla's altar? Could it be tampered with? How does she come in contact with the Elders? Did she know them personally? Betty was on a mission.

Chapter Nine

When Betty arrived at Layla's property, she waited in a small group of overgrown oak trees close to the house on the hill. It was in the back side so that Betty had a clear view of the kitchen, living room, parent's bedroom, the spare room upstairs, and Layla's bathroom. Layla was outside with Betty's ex-boyfriend, the one from the bay area. The place Betty had picked out, she was able to hear everything from that back patio. It echoed into the canyon.

Layla and that damn cheating boyfriend were talking about the Silver Spur. A place up in the mountains that was a clubhouse for adults to throw parties. Someone's birthday was coming up. They were going to attend it tonight. Nothing of real importance for Betty. She felt tired but dared not sleep. She wished she didn't take up Allen's advice to remember her dreams. She'd rather sleep in blackness.

Since Layla was going off to a party. Betty decided to come back later. She needed camp gear. She was going to camp out and watch. Then when the time was right, she'd hit Layla with the hard truth. Betty found a trail that led the back way towards the highway. Odd. Why was there a very well traveled trail this way? She took it and went towards town. She went to that small camper trailer. No roommate anywhere. Betty gathered up all that she could carry and headed back to the property of Layla's.

A small pump tent, a bedroll, some clothes, a few hygiene products, her black box of coven stuff, a flashlight, some food, and a wash cloth. She made camp where she could see that well traveled trail and the house. Summer school was over so she didn't have to worry about getting up so soon and leaving. But if there was a Coven meeting, she wouldn’t ever know about it. She had to follow Layla's lead on that. Betty didn't want to miss any meetings in fear of being assassinated.

The night came on fast out in the woods. A few cows moved about up some thin trails and up the mountain. Layla's step father could be heard yelling at Layla's mother. Layla must have left for that party earlier when Betty was gathering camping gear because she wasn't there. God, the screaming that went on in that house. It went on for about four hours into the dark of night.

There, Betty could see Layla. She was home the entire time. Where was she hiding out? Damn. Betty went to get a closer view moving stealthy in the tall dried up grass. Closer, closer. She made her way to the barbed wire fence by the huge giant oak tree and hunkered down by some low rising rocks. Layla was sitting there on the picnic table bench. She was reading in the dark. The kitchen light gave no justice to read in. What book was she reading?

A noise came from the drive way by the cattle guard. Betty was frozen solid. Hopefully it was just a cow. Her figure could be seen from that direction. She slowly moved to lay down on the ground. The rough grass cut into her bare legs. The dry dirt grinded into her hands and arms. Very gracefully she managed to lay down without making sound. Geez, how many people were spying on Layla? At the cattle guard was Allen. He had walked up to the fence and was staring at Layla. He just stood there. How long was this shit going on?

Betty started to sweat. She could feel it roll down between her smashed breasts. Sweat was coming down off her forehead. Why did she think of this? This was a bad idea. She put her head down in the dirt and with her arms, she covered her head. Betty started to wish she was somewhere else. Then she heard a door open. She looked up; it was Layla's step father. Betty glanced over at Allen. He was floating across the cattle guard. Or so it seemed. He walked over to the other side of where Betty was. More towards the front of the house, where Betty was more towards the back. Oh thank the stars in heaven he went that way!

His shape twisted and went down. Disappeared. Damn shape shifter. Where Allen once was, a cat jumped out from the tall dry grass. The cat walked up to the back patio. Layla's step father was talking to her about something. What? Betty couldn't hear the low voices. She was as talented as Allen. She had tried that shape shifting but she was too weak to do it. You'd have to be of a higher house of power to do such things. Betty's house of power was extremely low. She was only chosen as a "might be" Queen because of her ability to do future readings. They came fast through reflections. For others, it takes a while to predict the future. Too bad she couldn't predict her own.

The cat jumped onto the table and laid on Layla's book. Layla gently stroked the cat's fur. She rubbed his ears and under his chin. She knew exactly who that cat was. She was no fool about it. The step father went back inside and the lights went out in the kitchen.

"FUCK!" Layla shouted loudly. Then she went inside. The cat went around the corner of the garage.

Slowly the transformation twisted up into a black figure. Allen in human form. He stood there. A light flipped on again in the kitchen. Layla came out and sat back down. She looked around for the cat. No cat anywhere. She went back to reading her book.

Allen seem to have floated over to the parent's bathroom window and disappeared around that corner of the house. Layla closed her book and went inside. Where was she today? Betty got up from where she was laying and went over to the picnic table. The book was still out. Layla was in the kitchen. Where was Allen right now? What was this book she was reading? The bible. A noise. Betty quickly dodged under the table. There was no other place to run to. She looked at where the noise came from. Where the parents' bedroom was. There Allen stood in the darkness of the shadows. His back towards Betty. He was spying on her parents.

Layla shut the kitchen light off. Betty got out from under the table and peeped into the dining room window. Layla was heading upstairs. Betty tiptoed to the corner where she had seen Allen. She looked around that corner. Allen was still there. Good. Betty made her way to the front of the house and into the tall dry grass. Layla's bedroom light went on. She could see Layla undressing. The front door downstairs opened up.

Who was still up? Her step father. He was sneaking outside for what? Allen's shadow appeared at the corner of her parent's bathroom window. He was spying on the step father!

This was better than a soap opera! The step father stood out on the dying lawn and was watching Layla undress. Allen was watching the step father. Betty was witnessing the strangest thing right now. When Layla was finished, she turned off her light. Must have gone to bed. The step father went back inside. A television was turned on in the living room. The flicker of light was casting rays of colored light against the stairwell. Betty could see this perfectly through the distorted entry door window. Allen made his stealthy way to the front. He was standing right at the door looking in. How brave was that!

Betty wanted a closer look but dared not get close to Allen. She just stayed put where she was and watched. It must have been an hour or so that went by. Movement finally took place in the living room. A figure headed up the stairs. Allen quickly moved to the two stacked windows. The formal dining room window and up above that, Layla's bedroom window. He started to climb the stucco rock on the side of the house. Like a spider he moved fast for the prey up the wall. Allen tapped on the glass. Layla's light went on. Allen's figure disappeared as soon as she approached the window to open it up.

The figure going up the stairwell did a quick halt. It didn't move. Layla stayed at her window watching a moth float around in the light of her window. Betty shifted in the grass. The moth flew away and Layla heard something rustle out in the field. She must have heard Betty. She got up from the window and out her bedroom door. Where did Allen go? The dark mysterious figure that was frozen on the stairwell backed down and headed to the kitchen.

Layla's figure was now on the stairs. Then it was at the front door. She stood out on the front porch, closing the door behind her. She was looking out into the field. There, Allen was by a grove of trees behind Betty. Betty watched him move about to get Layla's attention. Layla headed in his direction. Strange, how the hell did he get down there by those trees? Betty felt frightened. The rush of being somewhere that she wasn't supposed to be. It could have an impact on the deception of what Allen had done.

Magic. Such a strange illusion for fools. Layla went down the drive way and over the cattle guard. Allen walked up from out of the field to meet her. Betty as quietly as she could move through the grass towards them so that she could hear what they were saying.

"Hey Layla." Allen said in such a somber tone. "Step father was about to make a move again. Thought you'd need your dark angel back by your window."

"I've managed without you Allen." Layla said a bit fired inside ready for a fight.

"I'm sorry." He apologized. "Look, I shouldn't have tried to piss you off. We're friends and I care for you."

"Broke up with Betty did you?" She said with the same temperament.

"No she left me today." He said. He didn't tell Layla why Betty left.

"Sorry to hear that. Did she hurt you?" Layla said actually concerned now.

"No. I hurt her." He said in a childish voice. "So, I am here with you." His head was down, his voice was low. Betty could still hear him. "I love you Layla. I'll never leave you again."

"Allen," Layla said, "I'm with someone right now."

"Break it off with that jerk!" He was getting angry. "He treats you like dirt Layla. You know that. He is a cheater. He's using you." Allen had truth in that.

"Alright Allen." Layla said calmly. "But if one thing

goes wrong between us, I'll kill you." She gave him a teasing smile.

"Not if I kill you first." He grabbed her hands gently and pulled her close to him. They kissed in the darkness of night. Their bodies had an aura of purplish hues and sparkles surrounded them. Betty felt her heart sink deep down to her stomach. She had absolute no chance to break them apart. Ever.

Betty got up without a care if they heard her and she went back over the barbed wire towards her camping spot. She entered her pump tent with disparity. Tears rolled down her cheeks. She flopped face down into her bedding. She cried herself asleep. Blackness fell around her like a comforting blanket of peace. She wasn't in the forest of hell but instead in a black hole. Sinking, sinking. Floating. Flying.

The next day came too early for Betty. The sun was brilliant and shining right in her face. The tent made everything a funky green color. She unzipped the stuffy tent and breathed in the fresh summer air. Dry but it felt better than the tent. She wiped the sleep out of her eyes. Betty observed around her. The trail, the field, and the back of Layla's house. There sitting at the picnic table was Layla's mom. Her step father's truck was gone. He was at work. Where was Layla? Damn, they wake up early.

Betty couldn't move out of her little area until the mom went inside. Betty had to clean up and get dressed. The creek was up and over the mountain. If she were to move now, she'd be spotted. So, instead of just sitting there, she rummaged around for a breakfast bar and a boxed juice. She pondered on what was said last night. Allen must have been there out in the fields every night until they got together. But why? Dark angel? As if Allen was anything but an angel. Betty giggled at that thought.

"I must have stayed up on that damn hill for about three months. I ended up being friends again with Layla but not with Allen because I was hurt." Betty softly said to Trent.

"Did you make it to any of the Coven meetings during those three months you camped out?" He asked.

"Yes. How the Mister found me is unknown. He was always at the highway where I had cut through the trail." Betty told him.

"About the trial," Trent questioned, "did anyone travel that trail?"

"I heard footsteps often on that trail but never seen anyone traveling it." She said. Betty started to wheeze. "I don't feel so well."

"May be you should get some rest." Ava said with tears swelling up in her eyes.

"No." Betty said as she coughed and shifted in the hospital bed. "If I go to sleep I won't come back."

Trent changed the subject of death. "So why are they after you now? Are you still in the Coven? Or did you get out?"

"I managed to get out once I found out about the white cloaked one." She said with her eyes closed trying to control the pain in her body.

"And what about the forest Betty? Did you ever

return to the forest?" Trent asked.

"I went back alright. I'm still there." She started to cry. Ava was weeping but tried to hold it in so that Betty would be able to tell about it.

Continuation school. New members of the Coven had joined. New assassins for the assassination bowl. The girls that hung in the forest by their necks disappeared from the face of the earth. Or at least this earth existence. No one talked about the disappearances of Skull County, especially when it involved witchcraft. It was covered up with lies of suicide, running away, and drug abuse.

The new members were mainly either at continuation school or drop outs. Heartless, spineless, and full of vengeance. This group of members had been strong. Layla was always disappearing with Allen but they never missed a meeting. Betty was rarely at school and was now living with her aunt. On Wednesday nights Betty, Layla, and J Dog would go out to the lake and party. They would drink all night long and then go back home in the early morning hours wasted off their butts.

Then one Saturday night as Chance, the obnoxious blond packed her car full of wild teenagers, including Betty and Layla, they headed off to an unknown party out in the foothills.

"Chance," Betty said, "I remember these guys we are going to meet up with." She was happy. Could have been the purple pills that she and Layla popped fifteen minutes ago.

"Yeah they say they are from the city. So let's show these city dogs what the country is all about." She laughed over the loud thumping bass of music.

The car unloaded as the pulled to a stop in front of a huge house. Every light in the house was on except for one window on the side. Music, kegs, grown men, young guys, teenage girls. The house was packed with moving drunken bodies. The smell of booze was pungent before you even walked up the walkway. The noise, the mayhem. Whose house was this?

Betty and Layla entered into the foyer. Looked around and then at each other. "Don't get lost Betty." Layla smiled.

"I believe I can find my way to the front door." She laughed. They were holding hands in a girly fashion.

"Well," Layla said, "they look all gangster. Be careful okay."

"I can take care of my own Layla." Betty smirked.

The girls then split up. Layla after some beer and Betty found one of the guys she had met with Chance. Betty was highly involved into a conversation with a guy when an older man approached.

"So how are you doing?" The older man asked. He was sober but artificially acted drunk. "Betty right?"

"Um," Betty said looking up at him standing by her, "yeah I'm Betty." She was a bit nervous.

The guy she was talking to looked up at the older man with a smile. Something was amiss.

"Come and drink with us. We are over here in this room having our own little party away from this racket and noise." The older man said giving out his hand to help her up off the sofa she was sitting on.

"Actually that does sound good." She smiled at both males.

They led her into the dark room. A few other gangster guys were in there already. They were talking and had their own private little set up with a keg they had rolled into the room.

"Drink?" One guy from the room offered.

"Thanks." She politely said.

She began another conversation with the small group and all seem to be good. Chance came in and started to get loud. The men didn't like this.

"If I can't laugh at your jokes than what the hell am I supposed to do dude?" Chance said.

"Be quiet woman cuz woman are to be seen and not heard." A gangster laughed rudely.

"Okay," Chance said with a hot note, "Betty our group is leaving this function. Let's go." She gave Betty the evil eye. "NOW!" Chance yelled.

Chapter Ten

Betty was shocked at how rude Chance was getting. Layla entered the room with the group that they came to the party with. Chance stood there by the doorway with her arms crossed. Her face was crossed too. That pathetic little scowl. Eyebrows knit. Trying to be something she was obviously not.

"Come on Betty it's time to go." Layla said in a firm tone.

"I'm not going with her." Betty said back.

"I refuse to leave Betty here Chance." Layla said to the chubby short blond.

"She isn't allowed in my car. Not after that." Chance gruffed.

"Chance. You have to take me home. You can't leave your friends behind." Layla said in a mature manner.

"Screw this!" and Chance stampeded out of the room. Layla and the others from their little group followed. Betty stayed behind with the gangsters.

"Well, now where were we?" Betty laughed.

"Drinking beer and talking about the hood." A guy said.

Betty was flirting with only one guy there. As soon as they started to make out, another guy wanted some of what Betty had.

"Whoa." Betty said as she pushed the other guy off her. "I'm a one on one type of gal." She smiled feeling slightly buzzed.

"But if he has you, so do we." The other guy said to her. He repositioned himself back to kissing her neck and playing with her hair.

"No no no." She said. "I don't think so." Betty got up from off one man's lap and tried heading towards the door.

"No no no." Another guy said repeating her. "I don't think so." He smiled cruelly.

"I have to go now." She smiled in an uneasy manner.

"When we are all finished, then you can go." Some other guy said. There were seven men in this room with Betty.

"Please don't do this." She said as she looked at all of them. "I'm only here because of the party. C'mon guys, I'm the cool one. Remember?" She begged.

"Yeah," one guy said, "the cool one always gives it up to all of us. You started to put out so now give it up."

The men surrounded her. They pulled the phone right out of the wall and used the phone cord to tie her to the bed. One guy took out a needle and some sort of spoon object. Two men ripped her clothes right off her body. Betty started to scream but yet another man tore up a piece of sheet and tied it around her head over her mouth. The man with the needle came up to her. He tied her upper arm.

"You won't remember a thing sugar pie." He laughed as he thumped for a vein. "Sweet dreams baby."

In went the needle. Her vein sucked it in like a dry dessert. Where the needle went in it had started to sting instantly. Betty was crying and struggling to get away from it. Her arm felt hot. It rushed through her body and her heart started to pound really hard. She was screaming through the choke hold of the sheet. Her body grew feverish. Flushed. Then everything went weak. She watched the men take off their pants. She was being gang raped. Her vision started to become blurred and she was ever so high on heroin.

Somewhere, somehow, Layla came through for Betty. She came into the room like a wild tiger. She hurricaned her way to Betty through all those men. She slammed the man who was one Betty against a wall and told him to die. When she let him go, he was choking and gasping for air. The others fled out the dark room, not wanting to mess with Layla.

"Betty. Oh my God." Layla was raged. "Come on let's get the hell out of here."

Betty was in and out of conscientious. "Layla." This was all Betty could say.

Layla untied Betty from the bed. Then she grabbed her friend and helped her walk outside to Chance's car. Chance didn't care. To her, Betty deserved it. Betty got into the car, Layla slipped in beside her.

"Drive you bitch!" Layla said to Chance. "I told you not to drive off. The next time this happens you will die like that guy in the room. Got it?" Layla's eyes were lime green. Layla took off her jacket and wrapped it around Betty's naked body.

"Take a chill pill dude." Chance said with a smirk. "Like it didn't happen before to her."

"It hasn't." Layla told her. "You do this again and I'll kill you."

Layla held her friend until Chance got to Betty's house. Betty was extremely out of it. Layla helped her inside and took her to her bedroom. Chance left the driveway. When Layla went back outside, she casted a spell where the car had been parked. She then walked out of the driveway only to find Chance having car problems down the road a few feet away.

Ever since then, it had seemed to be that Layla was rescuing Betty from men. Every time a party happened, Layla was there storming through a pile of men to help Betty. Betty felt that she was forever in Layla's debt. She fell in love with Layla. Men scared her because they only wanted one thing. That was pussy. She was vulnerable and now completely shy around a group of men. But when a man wanted her, she'd get tough because she knew Layla wouldn't be there all the time for her.

Betty was soon hanging out with an entirely different crowd and Layla was a hit and miss situation because of Chance taking all her time. Schellden Town was where she mostly hung out and at the Jeylind Graveyard at nights with her new found lover, Sophie. Sophie was a solitaire witch who begged Betty to leave the Coven. But there was one thing left at the Coven that had Betty curious. Who was that white cloaked demon?

Without having to follow and spy on other Coven witches, Betty and Sophie summoned up spirits on their own. Through crystal balls, tarot cards, and divination the white cloaked figure was called an Ancient. It was a male figure. A Prince from a foreign land. No one would ever know who he truly was. Just some guy who wanted earthly powers. The women were nothing more than a ploy to a greater plan. There was no such thing as a Hasbrath. Hasbrath was just a demon who messed with people's minds to get them involved, to believe, to be possessed.

Betty stopped going to Coven meetings out on Jesus Maria Road. She tried to tear up the book and burn it but the pages wouldn't burn. The next day, the book was gone along with the ashes of the black cloak and slipper shoes. The dagger, the other little trinkets, all gone. Disappeared.

Betty wasn't the only one who skipped out on Coven 82. So did Layla. She left town. The last meeting was when Layla left the Coven for good. Allen had lost his mind completely. He was in a state of un repair. Grunt disappeared and others followed that path. To get out. Some of the members stayed in hopes of being the "High Priest" or "Priestess". But no one could ever top Layla, Grunt, or Allen's powers.

"I stuck around for a while in hopes that Layla would return. She did a few times but then left out of state because The Mister was following her around. Her home life was beyond living for." Betty said to Trent in a weak voice. "In the forest," she told him as she grabbed her sheets to pull them over her cold body, "That hell I dream. Layla and this curly haired blond helped me take on my human form. I never saw Layla again in the forest. She was gone and I haven't seen her since." Betty coughed in pain. She was growing cold.

"Trent." Betty said trying not to go out on him. "Ava." She turned to Ava who was still holding her hand. "I've been clean and sober for six years. I didn't hurt myself."

Ava had tear streaks down her face. She asked Betty with a deep sorrow in her voice, "Who did this to you?"

"Someone in the Coven. A young man." She answered Ava in such horrible pain. "He couldn't take me down. I fought him every step of the way. He kicked the shit out of me, injected drugs into me, and then forced me to drink something in an old bottle. When these things didn't work, he then took me to the top of my apartment building. He took a noose, doused me in gasoline, threw me over the building and lit the rope on fire."

Ava and Trent were amazed. She lived through all of that. Even now living to tell of what had happened. A great sadness filled the room.

"Betty." Trent said. "Ava and I are going to pray over you. All I ask is that you accept Christ as your savior. That you believe He died for our sins and He rose again to save you." Trent said in such a soothing voice. "Okay?"

"I accept Jesus Christ as my savior." She told him. "I believe he died for me." Betty started to cry. Her heart space felt hot and on fire. "I believe that Jesus Christ rose again to save my soul from hell." She was weeping.

Trent and Ava took Betty's hands and they prayed over her. The Holy Spirit filled that death room with such heaviness that if any demon existed amongst them, it would've caught fire before their very eyes. The hand of God moved through Betty. It was so divine and beautiful. An aura of light hovered over her bed like waves of pastel ribbons.

This is me...

Hi there. I feel like this is one of those times that I need to introduce myself as a human rather than a character in some fairytale book. My name is Lacie Barg'e (last name pronounced bar -jay; it is french). I live in foothills. I was born and raised here. I have been raised a Christian and returned a Christian through the power of prayer. I've been in most of the states looking to fill in a "void" in my life but there was nothing that could accomplish that better than good old fashioned Church.

A little bit more about me. I was raised by a single parent (my mother) and with two brothers whom I love dearly but never get to see. They left the house when I was an adolescent and therefore I rebelled because I felt abandoned (and other disturbing issues). My entire family pushed me aside when I was growing up so I felt very alone and distant towards them. Today I am very close to my family, at least the ones who live near me. I have considerable amount of respect for them and hold them close to my heart today.

My stories of Skull County are not to diss my place of birth but to state the facts that there is indeed a Cult that resigns here. They have been here for about 100 years or so. The witchcraft that they practice isn't your ordinary Wicca or warlock type but a craft so powerful that it is about more than 4000 years old or so. I'm sure it was the very same "God" that Cain started to worship after being an outcast from God of Heaven. This dark God we would all know as Lucifer. Not to fear, Lucifer is very much earth bound. The forest in the dream realm tells us this. But he is looking for an able body to enter and possess since Lucifer can not come back as Christ did.

I wrote these stories to inform those who are seeking "Higher Power" and "filling in voids". I wrote these stories to tell the truth about a dark part of my life which I was never able to do before. The only twists in the three book series are:

- The book of the craft. Why? Well, it can't be found so therefore the language I can not disclose. I wouldn't have written the true language of the Coven anyway (in fear that someone might use it in curiosity) but it would have been nice to go and referance some of the rituals. Even though I am a Christian, I would still be able to read it where as others can not.

Why can others not read it? Well, I shouldn't say that no one can. A few can read it. Those who were chosen can read it. I'm sure Lucifer still wants my soul. He is like that.

- Names. All names of the people have been changed in my novels. Why? I am protecting them as they have protected me. When you leave a Coven, they will kill you. You shed blood for their "God" and so therefore you die for their "God". It is the way of their religion. I blended my friends (and even my own) personalities into each character so every character has a bit of all of us from

Coven 82.

- Places. Most places in my stories stayed but the real familiar places - names went back to their original names. I really wanted a part of the Gold Country history to take place in my three book series. It gives my true story a twist.

Other than that, what you read was real. I had gathered as much information I possibly could from ex-Coven friends and took my own experiences to write it. I can still remember what I experienced as if it had recently happened. The things I did and seen were so real, so strange and unbelievable that it knocked me in for a loop. I know that I am not crazy and everything was some sort of illusion. But it was so real that it frightened a lot of my former friends and family.

I now want to take the time to thank those who have helped me through this. One of them is my therapist. He has given me advice, strong sound advice and I was able to stand firm and write again. I thank God that I am still here and I'm excited to write more (less intrusive literature *giggles*, may be a romance or a children's book after this series). I want to thank a special friend out there who I am completely shy with (I know there is no need to be shy with you). This person helped me relax after a few days of restless nights of typing. My old friends that I got in touch with, your encouragement was a Blessing. My new friends that I met up with, your positive attitudes helped me focus towards a goal. Family members, thank you so much for loving me through my darkest hours.

When I was in the Coven, so many had prayed for me. I'm so thankful to have those prayers today. They helped me come back to the light of God. Today, I pray for those who are in darkness. It isn't a "in return" thing. It is something that moves my heart. If I can touch at least one soul that is lost into darkness, then I will know my job here is done. I'll be ever so thankful to do just that. My job with this story will be used in the greater good in my heart.

If I could turn back time, I'd have done things in life differently. But none of us can do that. It is now in the past. We learn from our mistakes and move forward trying not to repeat them and make them into a cycle. It has taken 11 years not to touch a tarot card, do palm reading, look into reflections and divination, or even burn things (plant life) on a make shift alter. Yes, two years ago I stopped doing these things. They got me no where in life. I'm much happier not knowing than I was knowing. Life has a meaning now. Sure I struggle, but it doesn't mean to turn to negative actions.

I enjoy life more and more each day now without having what I learned from the Coven intervene. I hope that all those who read these stories can find the same kind of harmony I have today. It is freedom to be yourself without another person's (or cult for that matter) influence who you are.

What the world won't tell you about cults....

I want to talk to you like I would an old friend. I'll be honest and up front about cults for I was in one. I say, ***was,*** because I am not anymore. In fact, there are only four survivors out of ten from the cult that I was in. Anyone who reads this book is a curious creature and you have an open mind for what is real in the world around us. I appreciate that.

As I was researching for that one book I was given 13 years ago, I could not find it anywhere. Not even on the Internet through Google. Which is not very surprising to me. It is an ancient book with words and symbols that I didn't understand back then. I was too naive and young. Today I understand what I seen and this frightens me. So many young adults who feel as if they do not belong are out there reaching for acceptance but not getting what they need to fit into society today.

Churches turn their eyes away from those who are different. I should know, I am one of uniqueness. The only religion that "feels" accepting to us is witchcraft and cults. Cults let us wear black, so it makes us "feel" secure, a cult can tell you the other side of the bible, etc. etc. What we don't know is it sucks us in to believing we have the power to control situations in our struggle to survive. We as humans have no power over any situation. As we all have heard before, "Shit Happens". Now it is the way in which we take it - negatively or positively. Negative is only going to bring more negative and positive is only going to bring more positive. That is our only choice in this world.

Cults are not going to let you actually know what they are about until you take their solemn oath. Every cult has an oath you take and usually these ceremonies are very secretive and on display for the High Priest, Reverend, a Pastor, etc... I guess you can say every religion is a cult of sorts. Even Christianity. But whatever "religion" you attend, you've got to ask yourself this one simple question: "Good or Bad?". Secrets are deep issues. They are bad. It is baggage you don't need. Being open (honest) has no issue attached. So, now I bring you the word which my novelette series stresses on.

The word cult. It means: to worship; reverential homage rendered to a divine being or beings. A particular form or system of religious worship; especially in reference to its external rites and ceremonies. Devotion or homage to a particular person or thing. By no means was I doing Wicca! No, there was no heaven either. This was (for me) an idea that held misfit teenagers into a place of acceptance. We were given tasks. We worshipped on a daily basis in our sleep and practiced our "craft" in our waking hours. Everyday we sought power to out do one another. The Elders of our group sought out a higher existence according to their "job" at hand by "Their Lord" (whomever that might have been).

There were times the ten of us would be totally afraid that one of us might lose our lives "according" to "Their Lord". The fact is, a cult like this, there was often blood shed. It was destructive. Sure the movies can make blood shed something fantastic. Tons of movies today are nothing but blood and violence. They are preparing you for this exact cult I was in. In reality (and not Hollywood style) have you ever smelled blood? Have you ever been forced to drink old blood? The real thing... Real blood? Yeah, most of you are saying "No but it sounds fun." Let me tell you - IT ISN'T FUN. In fact, your first taste of blood, guarantee you'll hork it up right away. And, the smell is so stomach hurling you'll wish that you never laid eyes on anything bloody. I'm not talking a prick of the finger, small cuts. I'm talking huge amounts to drown in!

Am I vegetarian? *Laughing here* I was for quite some time. Let's try a good eight years after coming out of the Coven, I wouldn't even eat a piece of meat (not even chicken). Cults screw with your minds. They have a way of making you feel like you are their greatest achievement. Take Betty in my story for instance. She had a vision after the fact she felt the need to get out. The Elders made her feel so needed that she stayed. She "thought" she'd be the chosen one. Now how special would that make a teenager feel? If your home life was miserable and now you might have the chance to be chosen, you would stay. Why? Because of curiosity. Because they were the only friends and family she had.

She wasn't a cheerleader. She wasn't the popular one out of the crowd. She was miserable and lonely. She was beat up by her father. She looked up to a misled friend who at first didn't want her in the Coven. Betty was directed into the Coven by a boy whom she had a crush on. The boy was misled by someone else. Humans also have the tendency to follow others who "seem" to have it all. All? What I mean by this is, power. Power of beauty, power of money, fame, fortune, happiness. Didn't Layla "seem" happy? Didn't Allen make Betty feel "loved"? Of course. So, she followed them.

Any cult/coven will seem wonderful. The truth is, they aren't. I really wish that Christian Churches would not turn away people based on looks, sin, or other information due to unfortunate circumstances in a persons life. If a person is seeking God, then by all means save the soul, flood them with Christ's love. Don't turn them away because of an issue. The reason I say this is because, yes I was in a Coven, I also have been turned away from Christian doors. I was not allowed in due to my fashion, due to my sin, due to my issues. I've been ignored by pastors, looked down on by mothers, and came face to face with the fear that God may never save me.

To me, those such Churches are cults themselves. I'm not saying that every church is that way. Some Churches were very accepting of who I am. They seen the change in my heart as I tried so much to heal from the Coven I was once in. They encouraged me to worship Christ. They prayed for me. They loved me for me. So, no, not all Churches are stupid. Just most. Today, and I'm just being honest, I belong to a Church that doesn't even know my name. Few members know me. But they don't call me and ask "why haven't you been to Church lately". It would be nice if there was a little concern for my well being. Tis okay, they are forgiven in my heart.

Cults are in fact political. They have their fingers in our police force, court systems, schools, and city boards. All these "mysterious" deaths and disappearances of young men and women (few children were involved) didn't just die without a cause. A young man last year committed suicide. He was an ex coven member. Strange that he killed himself. He loved his family, devoted to praying for others, and most of all had a love for life after hiding out for 10 years. Now why on earth would he pop himself off? To those that were in the Coven long ago and got out thought this was murder. Once you take that oath to be a part of a cult family, you are not to leave... EVER!

They will hunt you down. Why? They don't want you telling on them. Giving away their precious secrets. In order to ever leave a cult like the one I was in, you must die or give yourself up for sacrifice. Frightening, yes indeed. To be paranoid for the rest of your God given life, tracked down by an uncaring soul then erased by the hands of new cult members isn't a pleasant thought. I have lived in fear for 13 years. Some of you may be asking, "Then why did you write these tales?". Because I wanted everyone (especially you) to be aware of what is really out there. Today's television, movies, music, and etc. are preparing the world for cult religion. All that horror in these new movies, all the "okay" on violence and sex. It is a preparation of what is to come. Now for Churches to not accept those who seek light, these people who were seeking light will be accepted into a new dark order.

You don't have to believe me. I don't expect anyone to actually take any of this for granted. I just wanted you to be aware. Not everyone is a daisy out there. Not even me (although I would like to be one *smiles*). Cults will isolate you from former family and friends so that they can psychologically manipulate you into a state of fear. If you think for one minute that you don't fear them, I'd like to see you drugged, tied, and burned. "Oh but that won't happen, I'll kick their asses." Sure after they slipped you a mickie in your drink. Yes, they will use every nasty trick at you if you are the one that they will have spilling blood that night. Don't be a smart ass. We (and I speak for myself also) aren't so tough.

But I know of one thing that is tougher than the bonds of any cult/coven. It is prayer. Pray for protection. A sin is a sin no matter how deep and ugly it is. God will forgive you and protect you. How do I know this? Hello silly, I'm still alive aren't I? I'm more alive today than I ever was! My existence is living proof that God exists. Your existence is living proof that God loves each one of us no matter what fall we've taken in life. So pick yourself up from the rut and move those legs! Dance, feel free, be wild! (okay, not too wild because you might get arrested if naked in public *laughing here*). Feel it, believe it, get positive in it.

Cults won't let you do things that make you actually feel good. They make you feel lowly. In time, a cult will make you cower in front of other members. Again I use Betty as my example; she was turned into a bird. A small fearful creature in a dark forest of the dream realm. There in front of other Coven members she was turned into a small animal for all those to crush and hurt. Sure, we all would love to fly in dreams even in reality it would be lovely to fly around like a bird. But, there are dangers to being such a creature. Cats, dogs, cars, weapons. These things can kill a bird in an instant. Even the Dodo bird was killed by human hands, and I believe that may have been the biggest bird that existed on earth.

Birds are not protected in this forest realm of sleep like they are in real life today. Forget animal rights there. You suffered the consequences as they came. If you feared the mighty one in the forest, you were put to shame in front of a large group of followers. Your ego is smashed. It don't feel good to be put down and belittled. Then what happens after such an act? Revenge, jealousy, and hatred towards those in the cult. It just makes the issue of being in such a cult more ugly. The reality of it is this; joining a cult won't get you anywhere in life but into more trouble than you are already dishing out. It won't pay the bills, it won't put

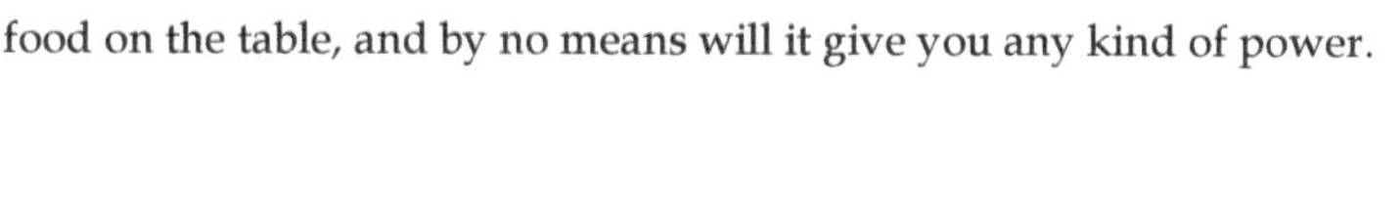

food on the table, and by no means will it give you any kind of power.

Society may be preparing us for cult activities now but in the end their will be something far more greater that will over turn the destruction here on earth. We battle this everyday of our lives and that is to keep our faith. Faith that we will achieve peace. Now don't you think the most oldest religion has a play in this? It isn't Cain. He was birthed into this world. It isn't Adam, the first existing man. It is your decision to look deep within and know in your heart what is the truth. Like I said, you don't have to believe me. The decision is your own.

www.ingramcontent.com/pod-product-compliance
Lightning Source LLC
Chambersburg PA
CBHW020944310726
48980CB00001B/44

* 9 7 8 0 6 1 5 1 4 6 7 8 2 *